Elaine's hands were working up Porter's calves. There was a period during which the only sounds were the little moans Porter couldn't bite back as Elaine expertly massaged her legs, her hands drawing nearer and nearer to Porter's groin.

Porter felt the wetness growing, and fought against it, to no avail. She was being seduced, and seduced well, and she knew it. When it seemed that Elaine could go no higher without becoming forward, she abruptly sat up, her knees between Porter's feet, her hands on either side of Porter's hips. "Do you want to go out now?"

Porter shook her head. She didn't trust her voice. Her stomach was a tumbling ball of heat, igniting and fusing everything inside her into one giant flame. Elaine smiled once more, then leaned over and kissed her.

Allergic Reaction

Leslie Adams

Cape Winds Press, Inc.
2000

Printed in the United States of America on acid-free paper
First Edition

ISBN 0-9671203-3-0

Library of Congress Number: 00-102131

Published by Cape Winds Press, Inc.
P.O. Box 730428
Ormond Beach, FL 32173-0428
http://www.capewindspress.com

Cover design by Mary Boone incorporating images obtained from IMSI's MasterClips/MasterPhotos© Collection, 1895 Francisco Blvd. East, San Rafael, CA 94901-5506, USA

To Cindy H, my inspiration

Chapter I.

Detective Porter Sienna cast silent dispersions upon Greensburg high society as she eased her car, a forest green Saturn, into a parking spot between two black and whites and nervously adjusted her shoulder holster. Summoning her best official grimace, she climbed out of the car and turned to face the front entrance of the Greensburg Country Club.

It had been at least seven years since she had been inside those doors. Seven long years. The building itself, a blinding white replica of an ante-bellum southern mansion, stood haughtily apart from the scurrying of the uniformed police and the crime scene unit, as if these intruders were beneath notice. Tall columns supported a covered entry through which a blacktop driveway ran. At the moment, the drive was blocked with a mortuary van and about eight police cars.

To her left, Porter saw the stairs that led down an embankment to the pro shop and the first tee. She could see golf carts dotting the course, white blips against a verdant green canvas. From the rear of the club came the splashing and laughter of children at the pool.

To the right, a dozen clay tennis courts ran the length of the parking lot, and the roof of the indoor courts could just be seen over the tall chain link fencing and black mesh that served to separate the courts from the cars. The parking lot was full of minivans, Cadillacs, Mercedes-Benzes, Jaguars and Rolls-Royces. Even the security guards drove Land Rovers, white with the green crest of the club emblazoned on the doors.

Running her fingers through her short red hair, Porter fought back memories of playing the golf course and swimming in the pool, of tennis lessons and formal dances, and tried to concentrate on the job at hand.

Looking at her watch, she noted the time, one forty-seven PM. It was a clear, warm southern day in early summer, and the North Carolina sun shining down made her feel overly warm in her slacks and blazer. Or was it just the sun? She felt almost nakedly exposed standing before the clubhouse, as if everyone inside knew she wasn't all that she seemed.

Beth had liked to sit in bed and watch her dress for the day's work, liked to laugh at the way she always studied herself to make sure she looked professional, looked straight.

Six months ago, looking straight had finally gotten the best of Beth. Now there was no one to tell Porter whether she was still getting the desired effect from her wardrobe; celibacy was easier than trying to keep another relationship.

Seven years ago, a twenty-seven year old Porter Sienna had shocked her father by announcing her intention to join the police force. The final act of the blow-up that ensued had been played out inside the front doors of the Greensburg Country Club.

Joe Graves pulled up in his Escort and got out. "Ready?"

Porter nodded absently at her partner, and the pair went together toward the entrance. Flashing their badges at the policeman standing watch, they passed through the heavy leaded-glass doors and into the exquisitely tiled rotunda. Porter remembered the last time she had stood in the round hall; she and her father had been arguing, and she had vowed she would never set foot inside the club again.

And she hadn't until that point. She wouldn't be doing so now, except she didn't know how the lieutenant would respond to her telling him she couldn't investigate the call because she had something against the effete snobbery of the country club of Greensburg.

Swallowing a snicker, Porter set her face and walked briskly toward the elevator. There was some small triumph in her return; it was expressly forbidden for women to wear pants on the formal dining level. Porter stuck her hands in her slacks pockets and grinned. *Screw their dress code.* She almost wished she were wearing polyester. *That would be the ultimate affront; a woman detective in a polyester pantsuit.*

The elevator doors opened, and Porter and Joe stepped inside the car. As the door closed, Joe let out a long breath and adjusted his tie. "Man, this place is the Ritz."

"Yes, it is. I wonder how many of us they could pay with what they paid to decorate that hall. I seem to remember that table cost around eleven grand." Porter remembered quite well; she had slammed her fists down on the very expensive inlaid mahogany and coco bola table repeatedly during that final argument with her father. Their voices had echoed along the rounded walls.

"I forget, you used to hang out here."

"Zip it," Porter growled. "Used to is ancient history."

The elevator stopped on the lower level where the locker rooms, pro shop and informal grill were located. The doors opened on a mob scene.

"Oh, Christ," Porter whispered. Joe echoed her

words. Swallowing, Porter smoothed her slacks and stepped into the hall.

She recognized far too many of the faces behind the cordon of police officers, friends of her fathers, friends of hers, once. She made her way toward the men's locker room, the last bastion of the southern white male, and hoped no one would recognize her. These people hadn't changed since 1952; on the other hand, Porter had changed immeasurably.

As she neared the doors leading into the grill, she got a prickling in her neck. Forcing herself to look up, she saw her father standing in the doorway with Susan beside him. Her father's second wife was another of the things they had fought about.

"Fuck," she muttered. "Fucking Christ."

"Porter!" Unwillingly, Porter stopped. Her father pressed forward. "Porter, wait a minute."

"Father," she acknowledged his presence. "You'll have to stay behind the line."

"Porter ... you look good." He seemed uncomfortable. "It's been a while."

"Yes, it has." She stared coldly at Susan, who quickly looked away. Her father shifted his stance.

"You should stop by the house," he said, then stopped talking. As Porter glanced around, she saw faces turning toward her, saw recognition dawning in more than one. People had started to realize who she was. This was the last thing she needed. Who knew how many of these people she would have to interview?

"I'm in the middle of an investigation, Father. Excuse me." Turning, she pushed her way through the knot of Crime Scene people and allowed the heavy wooden door to close behind her, shutting out the faces and the memories.

This was one place she had never been before. It had always held a magical, mystical quality for her as a child. Now it just smelled like any other men's locker room, like sweat, aftershave and cigarette smoke. And death.

"Jesus fucking Christ on the proverbial crutch!" Certain that no one outside could hear her, she let loose with the diatribe. Heads turned and the head of the Crime Scenes unit, Jennie Smyth, grinned at her.

"It doesn't smell that bad in here, does it?"

"I'm talking about them." Porter jerked her head toward the door. "Half those people I grew up around and the other half are probably getting the scoop on who I am right now. Trust my father to be around to make my life more difficult."

"That's what you get for being the Debutante Detective." Porter rolled her eyes and groaned. It was a nickname she'd picked up when she'd made detective and the newspaper had dug up her old debutante photograph, and it had stuck. She hated it. "Do you know this guy?"

Porter put her hands in her pockets and walked over to the body, looked down at the staring blue eyes and the messed graying blonde hair and shook her head. He could have been any one of a score of members of the club, all in their late middle years, all wealthy. It was a relief that she didn't know him. His lips were pale, his skin waxy and bluish tinged. He hadn't been dead very long. "Nope."

"Luke Williams, age 56. The men who were with him when he died ID'd him for us."

"Find anything interesting yet?" Porter glanced around at the officers scurrying about. Jennie shook her head and held up a plastic bag with a small medicine vial in it. There were traces of dusting powder on it.

"Just this and a used syringe. Could be a heart attack. Or suicide. But it doesn't feel right. Guy doesn't come in off the links, take a shower, and kill himself."

"Heart attack?" Looking at the well-cut slacks and white dress shirt, the silk tie that now hung to one side, Porter guessed it was possible. Luke Williams looked like a successful businessman who spent more time behind a desk than he should. His pants were unfastened. Bending over, Porter got a glimpse of what appeared to be silk boxer shorts.

She had several pairs of silk boxers herself. She just wished she had the nerve to wear them somewhere other than in bed. For a moment she felt a hatred of the dead man, that his life had been so simple and orderly, that he had been accepted, probably popular.

He had come in from playing golf and died. Then she reminded herself that she had made her own choices in life, knowing they wouldn't lead to an easy road. Jennie shrugged. "Possible. But we'll have to see what the ME comes up with. I'll put ten on accidental death."

"Keep it tight anyway. I don't want another mistake like Lee Street." She hadn't been in on that one, but the detective who had pulled the plug on the investigation had gotten busted for it. What looked like an accidental overdose had turned out to be murder.

"You know I don't work sloppy. I'll dust the damn floor for fingerprints if you want. But it looks to me like he just gave himself the wrong injection."

"What is that?" Porter peered at the bottle.

"Allergy medicine. I wouldn't think you could overdose on it, but I could be wrong."

"Well, we'll see. You don't have much for me to go on." Porter rubbed her temples.

"You like a puzzle."

"Great. Who's the officer in charge?"

"Morris." Jennie indicated a tall African-American man with her head. He was standing in a corner conversing with two other uniformed officers.

Porter studied the layout of the room, fixing Luke Williams' position in it. He lay just in front of a long lacquered wood bench that ran the length of the lockers, on a deep green wall-to-wall rug. On the wall

- 8 -

opposite him, a doorway led back to the showers. The walls were wainscoted in pine, with green paint above and a bold masculine wallpaper trimming the ten foot ceiling. The artwork was of golfing scenes and horses.

Strangely, it looked very similar to the women's locker room, which Porter had been in dozens of times. It was something of a let-down. She had always thought the men's room would be more masculine. She gave the place the once over, then started toward the officer in charge.

"Officer Morris," Porter said as she walked up to him. "Detective Sienna." Morris turned and smiled a toothy smile at her. His accent was thick and coastal.

"Well, if it ain't the debutante detective. You'd be my pick for this case." Porter managed to mostly contain her blush and forced herself to sound professional.

"Who was with Mr. Williams when he died?" Morris flipped through his notebook.

"There was a John Archibald, a Frank Simms, and a Philip Weakly." Porter let out the breath she had subconsciously been holding. She didn't know any of those names. "They'd just come in off the golf course."

"Where are they now?"

"The gentlemen's grill. I don't guess you ever been in there either, huh, detective?" Porter ignored him and turned to Joe.

"Find the director or whoever is in charge. We'll need an interview room set up. Tell him the card room will work just fine. I'm going to step outside for a minute." Jennie was doing a good job of overseeing the necessary procedures at the scene, and she and Joe would just be in the way at the moment.

Joe nodded and the two of them left the locker room. Joe went off upstairs and Porter studied the crowd. Her father was still there. Irritated, Porter turned her gaze deliberately from him and scanned the rest of the spectators.

Then she saw her. Taller than any of the women around her, her blonde hair short and curly, Porter felt instantly that she should know who the woman was. She was perhaps forty, though there were no detectible lines in her deeply tanned face. She wore a conservative business suit and little makeup.

Porter remembered to breathe. At the same time, the woman lifted her left hand to brush away an unruly lock of hair. A ruby red stone glittered on her pinky finger. Her blue eyes, a shockingly light blue, were locked on Porter's face, her expression seeming to say, *I know you're one too.*

Fighting the urge to turn around and flee back into the locker room, Porter instead moved with steady steps toward the gentlemen's grill. In reality it was a bar, and a place where women did not go. Porter felt the blonde's gaze boring into the back of her head as she walked with quiet determination into yet another no-woman's land. As she stepped through the door, she silently hurled an epithet at her father and took great pleasure in once again defying the traditions he held so dear.

*   *   *   *   *

The gentlemen's grill was empty save for the three men and a bartender. Porter frowned at the lapse in procedure that allowed the men to be here without an officer present. All four men looked at her as she came in with identical expressions of shock and surprise.

"I'm Detective Sienna," Porter stated in an attempt to assert her authority before anyone said anything. The bartender dropped his head and started polishing silver, and the three remaining men stared at her. They were similarly clad in khaki slacks and polo shirts, hair of varying shades of gray but mostly thinning, and tanned as golfers so often are. "I'll be in charge of this investigation."

"What investigation?" One of the men spoke up. "Luke just dropped dead. Had to be his heart. He'd been complaining - "

"I'll be taking statements individually, Mr. ..."

"Weakly. Philip Weakly." Porter made a mental note that of the three, Mr. Weakly looked the strongest. He had the air of a former athlete about him.

"I would appreciate it if you would not talk amongst yourselves until I have had the opportunity to take your statements. I don't anticipate it will take long, perhaps an hour." There was some grumbling. "I'm sorry for any inconvenience this may cause you, gentlemen."

She turned and walked out, motioning for a uniformed officer to join her outside the door. She instructed him to go in and prevent the witnesses from speaking about their statements, then looked for Joe. She didn't see him, but she did see her father. And the blonde.

The blonde was talking to someone. She suddenly glanced up and caught Porter staring, and slowly her lips curled up into a private and inviting smile. She raised her hand again, brushing at her forehead. Porter noticed that she didn't wear a wedding ring. Apparently seeing Porter's attention shift, then come back to her face, the blonde winked.

Blushing, Porter dropped her gaze and studied the thick carpeting. The last thing she needed was some rich society dame coming onto her in the middle of an investigation. Her thoughts were interrupted by Joe's arrival. He touched her arm and when she looked up, pointed toward the card room.

"We can set up in there. Are you okay? You look a little off."

"I'm fine. I just want to finish this up and get out of here." The two walked over to the card room and went in. While Joe opened his briefcase and got out FI reports, Porter paced the floor and wondered at the strange feelings charging through her body.

She found herself replaying the secret smile, the inviting curve of the blonde's lips, the glittering of the ruby pinky ring. The woman was a lesbian, that was obvious. But how had she known Porter was one as well?

"Well, who do you want to take first?" Joe asked. Porter pursed her lips.

"Weakly. Might as well start with him."

*   *   *   *   *

Philip Weakly settled himself into a chair and looked across the card table at the two detectives. Porter had decided to let Joe do most of the questioning, hoping that the men would relax more with him than they would with a woman.

"Your name, sir?"

"Philip Weakly." He shifted.

"Address?" Another shift.

"221 Rutledge." Porter whistled inwardly. Right on the third fairway, the prettiest hole on the course.

"Occupation?"

"Attorney." *Wonderful*, Porter thought irritably. *Just what we need.*

"How did you know the deceased?"

Porter felt herself tense. In the next moments, Mr. Weakly could go from a mere witness to something more. "We were golfing buddies." Had Porter detected a slight hesitation?

"You weren't his attorney?"

"No. I believe James Miller represented Luke."

"How long did you know Mr. Williams?" Joe asked the questions casually, as if he were filling out a questionnaire, which he was, in a way.

"Since we were children. We played together at Carolina." Porter had been right. Philip Weakly looked like an ex- football player. Luke Williams had not, but Weakly looked to have kept himself in much better shape.

"You don't seem to broken up over his death," Joe commented. Sensing that the interview was about to turn in the wrong direction, Porter interceded.

"We understand this must have been a shock. What can you tell us about the time leading up to Mr. Williams' death? You mentioned his heart." She shot Joe a look to silence him. He should have been able to guess that a society man like Philip Weakly wasn't the type to show his emotions, especially to police officers.

"We played golf. He started complaining of some pain on the eleventh hole. He took a pill, said he felt better. Anyway, we came in, showered, and were going to go to lunch. He was giving himself an allergy shot. He stood up to fasten his pants and all of a sudden, he just collapsed. He turned the strangest shade of blue ...."

"So there's no reason for you to suspect foul play?

He had no enemies?" Philip laughed.

"We all have enemies. But no, I don't suspect foul play. He had a bad heart."

"Thank you for your time, Mr. Weakly." Porter rose to shake his hand. He caught it and held on, studying her. Then, without another word, he dropped his grip and left the room.

"Next," Joe intoned in a stage voice. Porter stifled a grin and went to get John Archibald, a tall, thin man with glasses and a questioning air. Porter correctly guessed that he was a doctor, an orthodontist. She remembered her own set of braces, and shuddered. *The things women do for beauty.*

"Poor Luke. It was his heart, wasn't it. He didn't look so good around eleven." Dr. Archibald could give no new information on the deceased. They were only passing acquaintances, playing golf and socializing at the club, nothing more.

Frank Simms turned out to own the local luxury automobile dealership. He was an ebullient man, constantly gesturing with his hands.

"A damn shame," he expostulated for about the tenth time. "You know," he continued after a brief pause, "Luke had just bought himself and his wife brand new Mercedes convertibles. Burgundy with cream leather interiors, his and hers. Real beauties. And he paid cash for them, too! A damn shame!" He didn't appear to have anything else to say, corroborating what had transpired in the minutes before Mr. Luke Williams' untimely death, and so after taking his address and phone number, Porter let him go. She leaned back in her chair and looked over at Joe.

"Ten on accidental?" he asked.

"I don't know," she responded. "But I don't see any reason to keep the circus in town any longer. Let's wrap this up."

The men from the coroner's office were lounging against the lockers waiting for the crime scene people to get finished. When Porter and Joe walked in, they were greeted by the bright explosion of a camera flash. Blinking, Porter growled irritably at David Weems, the photographer.

"Hey, once in a while I like to take a picture of someone who's still moving." He laughed.

"I'll take an 8 by 10 glossy of that," Porter said, allowing herself to laugh with him. It was either that or start screaming. She took a deep breath. *Don't let this place get to you.* "You almost done here?" Weems nodded. "Okay. Wrap it up and get him out of here. We don't want to impose on these people any longer than we have to." Porter turned to the medical examiner.

"PM won't be until day after tomorrow. We're pretty booked up," he told her apologetically.

"Thanks, Ted. We'll be there with bells on." Porter hated attending autopsies. It wasn't the sight that bothered her but the smell. The smell was terrible.

But it was part of her job.

"I'll get this medicine to the lab ASAP," Jennie Smythe commented, coming over.

"He took a pill on the golf course. Check his bag and locker and send that down too." Jennie nodded. Behind her, the two coroner's office attendants were preparing to move the body. Porter stared at him a moment longer, then turned to her partner. "Okay, Joe, let's blow this joint."

Chapter II.

Porter stepped outside of the club and buttoned her blazer. For just a moment she wished she had a cigarette, then frowned. Giving up sex and cigarettes at the same time might not have been such a good idea.

"You realize pants are forbidden on the main level." The woman's voice was cool, but the edges danced with hidden amusement. Turning, Porter found herself captured in a pair of blue eyes.

"I'm afraid your dress codes don't matter much in a police investigation," Porter responded, hoping to sound stand-offish. She felt a need to put something between her and the blonde.

"So, what happened?"

"We're still investigating," Porter said automatically.

"Murder?" The blonde frowned and then answered her own question. She fixed her blue eyes unwaveringly on Porter's face and Porter felt her sense of balance shift precariously. "That's silly. If someone killed every person in this club who has stolen, bribed, or otherwise screwed anyone, there wouldn't be any members left." She smiled, a prize-winning smile that sent Porter spiraling off into fantasies that she didn't even want to think about admitting.

"What about you?" Porter forced her eyes to focus over the woman's shoulder and tried to return the levity she had heard in the woman's voice. "Have you ever stolen, bribed or otherwise screwed someone?"

There was no pause, only a short amused laugh. "If you believe my ex-, all three. I'm Elaine Jessup, by the way."

Porter shook the outstretched hand, noting the firmness of Elaine's grip, the solid looking muscle of her forearm. *Damn, this woman is good looking.* "Detective Porter Sienna. Sounds like your ex- doesn't like you very much."

Another laugh. "Well, she's a bitch."

Porter's breath caught. She had known it all along, but to hear Elaine admit it so easily was still almost a physical blow. Elaine laughed again, this time a hearty, full throated laugh.

"Why, Detective, I do believe you're blushing."

"I am not."

"Oh, yes you are. Now I suppose you're going to deny being attracted to me?"

Oh, Lord, what am I getting myself into? "You do believe in directness, don't you, Ms. Jessup?"

"Yes. I'm attracted to you. What do you propose we do about it?"

Porter fought for control. She didn't dare allow this woman to know ... "I propose we do nothing about it. Your sexual orientation isn't any of my business."

"Too bad. You're pretty good looking for a cop."

And you're pretty good looking for a society snob. "Thank you, Ms. Jessup."

Elaine crossed her arms and cocked her head at Porter, who fought against drowning in her light blue eyes. "I know you."

Porter's heartbeat tripled, and she swallowed hard. "I can't imagine ...."

"You went to Greensburg Prep, didn't you? You're Blaine Sienna's daughter." Porter sighed her relief and nodded. "Oh, yes, the Debutante Detective. I should have known. Well, Detective Sienna, may I offer to buy a fellow alum a drink? No strings attached."

"I don't get off duty until five on a good day," Porter replied. "And it may be a late night today."

"Then take my number." Elaine pressed a piece of paper into Porter's hand. She glanced down at a cocktail napkin. Below the green crest of the country club was a number written in black ink. "I'll be home after five-thirty myself."

Porter studied her. It would be nice to have a drink with a good looking woman. She didn't need to reveal her own preferences just to have a drink. She slipped the napkin into her pocket. "Yes, I suppose that

- 20 -

would be all right. Unless I'm too late getting in."

Elaine's smile broadened and she nodded. "That sounds fine." She walked off, her hips moving in a hypnotic side to side motion.

"Well, ready to break the news to the widow?" Joe startled her out of her examination of Elaine Jessup's shapely legs. Sucking in a breath, Porter turned and faced him.

"I suppose. Want to take my car?" Joe nodded and Porter fished in her pocket for her keys. As she started down the steps, Elaine pulled up in a silver Jaguar and honked the horn.

"Don't forget to call me!" She drove away. Her vanity plate read 'IDAREU'. Blushing, Porter turned to Joe, who pretended sudden interest in the marble column nearest him.

"School chum," she muttered. She and Joe had only been partners for nine months, and he seemed happy to ignore her personal life all together, which was fine with Porter.

"Good looking one," Joe said, taking a peek at the departing sports car. "Too bad I'm married."

"You old goat." Porter trotted down the steps with Joe in tow. She suppressed a grin as her taller, broader companion folded himself into the passenger seat of her car, then slipped the key into the ignition and backed out. "Well, let's hope we don't end up with a screamer on our hands."

"She'll probably just pour herself a scotch and say

'So?'" Joe let out a short laugh. "I doubt there are many happily married couples around here."

Silently, Porter echoed his sentiment. She put the car in gear and aimed down the long driveway toward Hawthorne Road.

* * * * *

The Williams house was three long blocks away from the club, overlooking the fourteenth green. When they pulled into the sloping drive, even Porter had to whistle. She knew the house well, as it was one of the largest on the road, but she had never had a reason to stop and study it.

Three full stories of brick, tall windows with black shutters and white frames, tall shrubs well manicured and set in neatly kept flowerbeds along the foundation. The driveway curved around behind the house, but Porter stopped at the brick walkway leading to the large double front doors.

The yard was immaculate, green, with islands of ivy and daffodils here and there. A small sign by the walk indicated which yard service maintained the landscaping. Sighing, Porter adjusted her shoulder holster and got out of the car.

"How much you figure this place is worth?" Joe asked quietly as they approached the door. Porter shrugged.

"A million, maybe one and a quarter, if there's a

guest house."

"Shit!" Joe whistled and adjusted his tie. He slicked back his hair with one hand while reaching for his identification wallet.

Porter withdrew her own leather case and flipped it open to reveal her badge and ID. They climbed three steps to a wide porch, then Porter pressed the doorbell. A deep resonating chime sounded.

The door was answered by a black woman in a maid's uniform. Porter grimaced to herself. "May I hep' you?"

"I'm Detective Sienna of the Greensburg Police Department. Is Mrs. Luke Williams at home?" The maid studied the two of them for a long moment.

"Come in. Miz Williams jes' got home. I'll tell her you're here."

Porter and Joe followed the woman into a lavishly furnished living room. Porter's experienced eye took in the antique furnishings and original gallery quality art. Joe, meanwhile, was looking for somewhere to sit. There was a fireplace with a carved wooden mantle, and over it hung an oil painting of a distinguished looking woman in her forties or early fifties.

Five uneasy minutes later, the model of that painting walked into the room. Mrs. Luke Williams was perhaps five feet six inches tall, with salt-pepper hair and piercing green eyes. She had a regal face, long and thin, and the svelte body of a woman accustomed to exercise. Her dress was conservative

- 23 -

and expensive. She waved a diamond studded hand in Porter's direction and smiled.

"What can I do for you, officers?"

"Mrs. Williams?" Although Porter knew instinctively that is who the woman was, she was still obligated to clarify the identification. The woman nodded. "I'm Detective Sienna, this is Detective Graves. I'm afraid we have some bad news."

The woman went white. One hand clutched nervously at a strand of pearls that circled her neck, the other reaching for the back of a nearby chair. Her stance seemed almost posed to Porter, but the shock in her eyes was real enough. "What's wrong?"

"Your husband is dead, Mrs. Williams." There was no soft way of saying it, no socially polite form to be used to tell this commanding woman that her spouse was deceased. Mrs. Williams stared at the two detectives for a moment, and then sank down into the chair she was holding. "I'm very sorry to have to tell you ...."

"How?" Her voice was almost a whisper. "What happened? Was it – his heart?"

"We are still investigating the cause of death," Joe said, looking uncomfortable. "At this point we aren't sure –"

"It had to be his heart." Mrs. Williams lifted her head and stared directly at Porter. There was a strange inflection in her voice, a determination. "Would either of you care for a drink?"

"No, ma'am." Porter answered her succinctly, then watched as she got up and crossed to a portable bar in the corner. Pouring herself a generous glass of something amber out of a crystal decanter, she replaced the stopper and took a sip before turning around.

"Did he ... did he suffer?"

"Death was relatively instantaneous," Joe responded. "We will need you to come to the morgue and make a positive identification ...."

"Yes, of course." Mrs. Williams seemed to be regaining her composure. "When did this happen?"

Porter consulted her watch. "About two hours ago. If we may, we need to ask a few questions for our report."

Again, Mrs. Williams stared at her. Then she smiled a small, lost looking smile. "Of course, dear."

"Mr. Williams gave himself an injection just prior to his death. Was he under doctor's orders to take some sort of medication?"

"Yes. Allergy shots. Luke has ... had ... terrible allergies. But he had taken a shot from the same vial this morning, unless he took a new vial with him. But he wouldn't, not with that one still not empty."

"What was your husband's occupation?" Joe was making notes, trying to be unobtrusive.

"Investments. He had his own company."

"I take it he did well." Porter's tongue tripped over asking the question. Her upbringing rebelled against asking questions about income and wealth. It wasn't polite.

"Yes. He has been having a good year."

"What do you do, Mrs. Williams?" Joe sounded conversational, trying to put her at ease. She turned a raised eyebrow to him.

"Why, nothing. I volunteer a few hours a week, serve on a few committees here and there. I have just gotten back from the hospital, as a matter of fact." She seemed to be back under control of herself. "When will the body be released for burial? I'll need to make arrangements."

Noting that she had not yet shed tears, and thinking it a little unusual, Porter said quietly, "There will have to be an autopsy. I think tomorrow evening at the earliest."

"An autopsy?" Surprise showed clearly on Mrs. Williams' face. "Whatever for?"

"In cases of sudden death, an autopsy is required," Joe intoned, taking the position of explaining the red tape. Mrs. Williams opened her mouth, closed it again, and turned appealingly to Porter.

"Detective Sienna – surely no one suspects foul play? Why, Luke doesn't have an enemy in the world!"

"I don't mean to sound impolite, Mrs. Williams, but did your husband have any reason to want to kill himself?" Porter bit her cheek in disgust at having to withstand this conversation. It was easy when she was talking to an ordinary person, but Mrs. Williams was 'Society', and all of her upbringing rebelled at the intrusiveness her job required of her.

"Suicide? My God, no." Her eyes wide, Mrs. Williams looked between the two. "No reason whatsoever!"

"I see." Clearly, Mrs. Luke Williams wasn't going to be forthcoming with anything useful, and Porter wanted to get back to the station and finish her paperwork. To her shock, she found that she was anxious to get home to call Elaine. "Thank you for your time, Mrs. Williams. Will you be able to come down to the morgue soon?"

"Immediately. Of course."

"I'm very sorry at your loss." The words sounded stilted, but Mrs. Williams accepted them with a quiet nod of her head.

Porter and Joe were almost to Porter's car when she realized she hadn't even gotten Mrs. Williams' first name. As they backed down the driveway, Joe flipped through his notes. "What did you make of her?" His tone was bored.

"Cool. Very cool. Probably trying to decide which dress was appropriate for identifying a body. I don't think she loved him very much." Porter felt an irrational anger. The only couple she had known as a child to be truly loving and devoted to one another had been her own parents, and death had broken that happiness up far too early. When her mother died,

Porter was just eighteen. It was the beginning of the end as far as Porter and Greensburg high society went.

There was silence during the few minutes it took to drive back to the club. Porter let Joe out of the car, then headed downtown toward headquarters. It had been a long day.

Chapter III.

At five-twenty, Porter turned her car out of the police station parking lot and toward home. She wanted a shower and some company, and Elaine Jessup seemed just the person to satisfy that want.

Somewhere between downtown and Forest Hill, a distance of ten miles, Porter found herself wanting more out of the evening than just a drink. Elaine moved in different circles than she did; it wasn't likely they knew any of the same people. There wouldn't be any risk of being outed.

Groaning, Porter knew that it didn't matter what lofty aspirations she held toward celibacy; she missed a woman's touch. Missed it enough to want nothing more than to jump at the chance to have it again, even if it meant a one night stand with a rich society snob like Elaine Jessup.

Inside her condo, she stripped off her blazer and tossed it over the back of the sofa. Picking up the phone, she fished in her pocket for the now-rumpled napkin and dialed the number written on it. Elaine answered on the third ring.

"Hello," she said, sounding casually pleased. "I was wondering if you'd call."

"Well, I wondered myself for a while." Porter started pacing, the cordless phone tucked between her ear and shoulder. "Did you still want to – go out?"

"Yes, I would. How about I come over and pick you up?"

"I – sure, why not?" Surprised with herself, Porter thought desperately for some way to take back the words. Elaine laughed over the phone, a musical noise that aroused Porter's baser hungers.

"Well, give me your address." Porter did. "I can be there in half an hour."

"Yes. All right. I'll see you then." Elaine broke the connection and Porter listened to the dial tone for a moment before hanging up. She went and took a shower, anxious to rid herself of the scent of death that clung to her. Perhaps no one else could detect it, but she could.

Afterwards, she surveyed her closet for clothes to wear. She wanted to look good, but not too good. It had been so long since she had been out. Lately, work was the only thing that kept her going. Beth had been the one with friends, and those friends had left with her.

Not that Porter minded so terribly; Beth had been a drinker, and her taste in friends hadn't exactly coincided with Porter's.

Snotty, Beth had called her. Porter had just shrugged and let the accusation go unchallenged. Maybe she was a snob. She saw no reason to hang around with people whose favorite pastime was building pyramids of empty beer bottles. Beth had been different in that at least, or had she?

Not wanting to think any more about her failed relationship, Porter selected a pair of light gray cotton slacks and a light olive silk blouse. She dressed absently, her movements automatic as she styled her short hair in an upsweep that lifted it off her forehead and made her look, in her opinion at least, like Brigitte Nielsen in Red Sonja.

Same hair color, she thought sourly as she applied what scant makeup she used, *but the rest of the body could use work.* She had harbored a secret and major crush on Brigitte Nielsen for a long time, and it was no surprise that she found herself constantly attracted to tall, muscular women.

The doorbell rang as she finished dabbing herself with perfume. Taking a deep, bracing breath, Porter went to answer it. Elaine stood in the doorway, smiling. She had changed into a pair of black slacks and a white camp shirt. A pink sweater was tied around her shoulders.

"Come in," Porter said in what seemed to her a very small voice. "I'm almost ready to go. Meanwhile, make yourself comfortable. If there's anything left in the bar you're welcome to fix a drink."

"Do you live with someone?" Elaine picked up one of Beth's shirts and dropped it on top of the box it was supposed to be in.

"Not anymore." Porter turned away. "She just hasn't had the courtesy to get the rest of her shit yet."

Elaine moved to the bar. Porter heard her fixing a drink. There was a pause. "So, Detective Porter Sienna; is there any basis to the allegation that you're a lesbian?"

This is where I cross the line, Porter thought. Aloud, she tried to sound casual as she said, "I agreed to go for a drink, didn't I?"

"That doesn't mean anything. Maybe you're just curious." Elaine moved to the sofa and sank down, crossing her legs in the Junior-Cotillion class approved way, ankles crossing, knees together.

"If I was just curious I'd certainly choose someone less open than you are." Porter was beginning to think this was a mistake. A big one. Elaine obviously didn't care who knew she was a lesbian.

"I guess you have to be pretty careful in your profession." Elaine seemed sincere as she leaned forward.

"Yes."

The two women studied one another for a long moment, then Elaine laughed and stood up. Crossing to the stereo cabinet, she bent her head to study the CD's. Porter watched her with a growing desire she couldn't quite understand. A moment later, Elaine looked back at her and gestured with her hand.

"Go on, finish getting ready. I'll be fine. I won't steal the silver while you're in there."

Porter went. As she stood in the bedroom, studying herself in the mirror and trying to steady her senses, she wondered once again if perhaps she were making a mistake. She could still head things off by getting the two of them out the door and somewhere where there were other people.

When she returned to the living room, Elaine had dimmed the lights and put a CD in the player. Soft music emanated from the stereo speakers. Elaine came to her and handed her a drink. She took a sip; bourbon and water.

"How did you know?" She held the glass up and Elaine shrugged.

"The bourbon was almost full. Everything else was almost empty. That told me you either hated bourbon or had just replaced it. I took a chance. Besides, you look like a bourbon and water kind of woman."

"Hmm. I thought we were going out for a drink."

Elaine studied her with the same inviting smile that had first gotten her attention and Porter felt herself melting. "We can still do that if you want. I thought you looked like you could use a quiet evening in."

I've had too many quiet evenings in, Porter wanted to say. *I want to go out where it's loud and crowded....* "Yes," was all she could manage.

"Good. Come over here. You look nice."

"Thank you." Porter crossed to where Elaine was patting the sofa. She sank down onto it and took a drink.

"How about a foot rub? I find those particularly relaxing after a long day at work." Before Porter could answer, Elaine was on her knees, removing Porter's pumps and massaging her feet with strong hands. Porter groaned at the pleasure.

This is unreal, she thought. *I'm sitting here with the most beautiful woman I've ever seen massaging my feet....*

"What do you do?" Porter asked, trying to keep her mind off the image of Elaine's naked body astride hers. Elaine shrugged.

"Investments. Boring stuff. Not nearly as exciting as being the debutante detective must be."

"I hate that nickname."

"I can understand that. I won't use it again." Elaine's hands were working up Porter's calves. There was a period during which the only sounds were the little moans Porter couldn't bite back as Elaine expertly massaged her legs, her hands drawing nearer and nearer to Porter's groin.

Porter felt the wetness growing, and fought against it, to no avail. She was being seduced, and seduced well, and she knew it. When it seemed that Elaine could go no higher without becoming forward, she abruptly sat up, her knees between Porter's feet, her hands on either side of Porter's hips. "Do you want to go out now?"

Porter shook her head. She didn't trust her voice. Her stomach was a tumbling ball of heat, igniting and fusing everything inside her into one giant flame. Elaine smiled once more, then leaned over and kissed her.

Porter's mouth opened under the quiet insistence of Elaine's lips. She felt the melting heat in her stomach spreading throughout her body, catching her off guard and sending her spiraling into a hungry desire that quickly overwhelmed what little reserve she had left.

Elaine's mouth seemed to be everywhere at once, on her face, her neck, her tongue tracing lines of fire that burned even after it had moved on. Again their lips met, parted, and Elaine's tongue searched the inside of her mouth.

Porter gave a little groan.

"The starch detective unravels a bit," Elaine teased breathily, exploring the curve of Porter's ear.

"You talk too much," Porter replied, turning her head to recapture the velvet lips.

Elaine's hands came to Porter's neck, moved into her hair. They kissed long and slow, until the need to breathe parted them. Elaine's fingers trailed down the length of Porter's sinewy neck to her shoulders, then curved farther.

Questioning fingertips circled inward around breasts that strained upward to meet their teasing lightness like flowers rising to the sun. Porter felt again the surges of desire that drove through her, waves on an incoming tide. She lifted her arms around Elaine's waist and pulled her closer.

Elaine began to unbutton Porter's blouse. As each button fell away beneath her fingers, she pulled the fabric open a little farther until at last the whole of Porter's chest lay visible. The lacey pink bra fastened in the front, and Porter held her breath when Elaine's hands, sure now, came to the clasp.

Elaine looked down at her, studying her intently for a long moment, then slipped an arm beneath her and lifted her, divesting her of her blouse and bra with the other. Rotating, she pressed Porter into the thick Oriental rug that lay in front of the sofa.

Porter lay acquiescent, wondering that she could be so compliant, so willing. She wanted Elaine with a desire that boiled amid the suppressed heat of long months of celibacy, and with a passion that defied any attempt of comparison.

She had never wanted another human being the way she wanted Elaine.

"Do you remember the first time you realized how beautiful a woman's breast was?" Elaine seemed fascinated with Porter's breasts, her hands caressing them, fingers softly following their curves. The fact that her actions were making the nipples harden seemed lost on her.

"You do talk a lot." Porter felt off-balance between the raging hunger that Elaine had fired and the subtler, and possibly far more dangerous, arousal her touch was bringing.

As if dragging herself from some dream, Elaine looked at her face, her eyes glassy. Slowly, she reached up and put a hand on Porter's cheek and smiled. "You're beautiful."

"Thank you." Elaine bent to her, kissing her again with a soft mouth that slowly hardened in passion. Her hands now sought the erect peaks of Porter's breasts, squeezing and rolling them, experimenting until the movement of her fingers brought another moan from Porter's lips. Elaine's tongue, quick and hot, moved down her neck to the hollow of her throat, teasing, licking, tasting. Farther down, to her breasts.

Porter pressed herself upward as she felt Elaine's mouth on her, moving toward her nipples with barely restrained eagerness. Her hands wove into Elaine's short hair, guiding her head.

Elaine's tongue reached out and touched a nipple, then there was a delicious moment when her breath came hot onto Porter's wet flesh before she lowered her face and took the nipple into her, suckling with the vigor of a newborn.

Porter groaned her hunger and closed her eyes, giving herself to the feelings coursing through her from chest to thighs. Elaine's hand closed around her other breast, kneading it gently in time with the movement of her lips. She moved back and forth between the two, sucking with little noises from deep within her.

Urgent need rose within the blossom of desire, and Porter took Elaine's hand from her breast and brought it to her mouth. Her lips touched each finger, brought it into her mouth before she drew it back out, slowly, her tongue dancing on the fingertip. Elaine moaned softly, the sound vibrating against Porter's breast.

Asserting herself, Porter rolled over, astride Elaine's Izod slacks. Her hands moved with steadiness to unfasten the cotton blouse. Elaine wore a chemise underneath in place of a bra, and Porter slipped it over her head even as her lips sought Elaine's. Their bare breasts came together, Porter's wet from Elaine's mouth.

Elaine's smaller breasts were tautly erect, the large puckered brown areolas thrusting her nipples upward against Porter's chest. Porter slipped between Elaine's thighs, knelt there, and bent to take a nipple in her teeth.

The taste of her skin was salty, tantalizing with the faint odor of her musk, foretelling of what other tastes lay below. Porter savored Elaine's breasts as she rolled her face against them, her mouth busy on the nipples. Porter's fingernails raked upward along her spine and across her shoulders, then her palms pressed against the shoulder blades, pulling her in.

"I need you naked," Porter whispered, her hands moving to the buckle of Elaine's belt.

"Take me to your bed." Elaine took her hands away

and pushed her up, standing with her. They kissed closely, hands warming the skin of each other's backs. Then Porter led her to the bedroom and turned back the covers.

"Take off your slacks," she ordered. Elaine unfastened her belt and pants, and pushed them down over her hips. Her briefs were high cut and cotton.

"You take them off."

Porter knelt and pulled the slacks down to Elaine's ankles. Lifting her head, she breathed deeply of a more powerful scent of arousal. Then she leaned forward slightly, her breath stirring through the cotton fabric that separated her lips from Elaine's mound.

Elaine's thighs quivered noticeably. Porter stood, then dropped her own slacks and stepped out of them. They looked momentarily at each other, then Elaine cupped her hands around Porter's buttocks and pulled her in, kissing her forcefully. Porter's desire exploded at her touch.

They fell across the bed, intertwining arms and legs as the passion built. Elaine's hands moved with practiced expertise along the lines of Porter's body, teasing her with their lightness, tormenting her with sudden pressure at sensitive moments.

Porter fought to keep control of the situation, to control their lovemaking as she had with every other lover, but Elaine overpowered her with her mouth, her fingers, her body. After a very long time, Elaine raised up and took in the length of Porter's body, her eyes bright.

"I want you."

"Take me." Porter had lost any battle they were fighting. She lay waiting, wanting to be touched. Elaine smiled softly and slowly pushed Porter's briefs down over her hips. Her fingers were light brushstrokes across the curly blondeness of Porter's hair.

Porter groaned and pressed her hips upward. She didn't think she could wait any longer. Elaine moved into her wetness at the same time she dropped back down on top of her, her fingers sliding between Porter's swollen lips as easily as if they had been there a thousand times before. With her free hand, she pulled at Porter's underwear until Porter was able to wiggle them the rest of the way down her calves and off.

As soon as Porter's legs were free, Elaine applied gentle pressure with her knees, spreading Porter's thighs wide apart, and found the source of her wetness with practiced speed. Her fingers danced against Porter's skin for a brief moment, then plunged with a single thrust deep into the heat of Porter's passion.

"Oh, CHRIST!" Porter almost screamed the words as pleasure spun out from Elaine's hand, as her slick walls parted and filled with Elaine's fingers, tugging at them, welcoming them in. Her hips strained upward of their own accord, meeting each thrust with their own counter-thrust.

Elaine grinned hungrily and moved her other hand into Porter's hair, tangling it through her fingers and gripping tightly. Her lips moved down Porter's neck to suckle at her breast. Porter sweated and groaned her desire, her hands pulling Elaine's mouth hard against her. She felt the surge of orgasm building, felt it rush forward against Elaine's hand only to fall back and rush again, more forceful, more insistent.

Again and again, a rising tide of need, until at last her desire crested and broke, and she went spinning into a long, wailing climax that drained the energy from her very soul to sustain itself in unbroken contractions.

At last, Porter's back relaxed and she fell against the bed, unable - unwilling - to move. Elaine kept her hand still within her, her kisses turned soft and undemanding as she curled up next to Porter and smiled over at her.

"Did you like that, Detective?" Porter groaned a response. Elaine moved her hand slightly and smiled more broadly when Porter jumped and drew in a sharp breath. "I think the detective liked it."

"God damn if you don't talk a lot," Porter managed. "Come here and let me see if there's anything I can do to shut you up."

Elaine laughed and complied.

*   *   *   *   *

Porter woke to the sound of the shower running. Rubbing her eyes, she looked across the room at the luminous numbers on the clock radio: 5:45. In fifteen minutes the alarm would be going off to tell her it was time to get up.

The shower stopped and a minute later Elaine walked out into the bedroom, a towel wrapped around her waist. Her full breasts were still beaded with water and her hair was tousled and unruly.

"Good morning, detective," she said, smiling softly. "How did you sleep?"

"Stop calling me detective," Porter growled. "I've got a name."

"Yes, I know. Did I wake you?"

Porter nodded. "But I'd have to get up in fifteen minutes anyway. May I fix you breakfast?"

"How about I fix it while you shower?" Elaine was getting dressed, a process which Porter was disconcerted to realize aroused her as much as watching her undress had been. She forced her attention to the wall and swung her legs out from under the covers.

"All right."

Porter's shower was short. As she soaped up, she remembered the way Elaine had looked at the height of her ecstasy; the soap slipped from between her fingers and hit the shower floor.

"Damn," Porter mumbled to herself, bending to retrieve it. "Of all the times to get a raging case of lust...." She quickly rinsed off and went to get dressed, hoping that a cup of coffee would restore her senses.

She stepped into the kitchen to see Elaine setting the table with two plates of bacon, eggs, grits and toast. "Do you dress that way all the time, or are you trying to impress me?" Porter glanced down; she had chosen one of her best pants suits without realizing it.

Caught, she shrugged and tried to laugh it off. "Oh, this old thing?"

"Yes, that old thing. Sit down and eat before you start to get strange on me." Porter sat. Elaine poured the coffee, then sat next to her. They ate for a while in silence.

"I enjoyed myself last night," Porter finally said to break the silence. "Thank you. It's - been a while."

"I could tell. Thank you for letting me be the one."

"What?" Porter looked curiously at her.

Elaine smiled and pushed an unruly lock of hair out of her face. It was a gesture that Porter was coming to find endearingly attractive. "You act like you're in some kind of self-imposed exile from women. I'd guess that your former lover is responsible, and I'm glad you let me be the one to break you out of it."

Porter blushed. "It's not so much exile as ... well,

relationships are difficult. Difficult to come by and difficult to keep. You slipped past my guard last night. Properly prepared, it would never have happened."

"Well, even so. You have my number; maybe we can go out again sometime. I don't expect an invitation to move in." Elaine curved her lips into a smile over her coffee cup. "You're very good at what you do."

"I like to think I'm a good cop." Porter blushed more deeply, being deliberately obtuse.

"I wasn't talking about that."

"I know." She coughed. "Maybe we can go out this weekend. I – ah – maybe...." She trailed off and took a bite of toast to cover her confusion. She wasn't accustomed to such directness. It worried her at the same time it excited something in her which had until that point been dormant.

"I should go. If I don't stop at home and feed Antigone, I won't have a sofa left by this afternoon." Elaine finished her coffee and stood up. "Well, detective, call me later?" She crossed to the small dry-erase message board by the refrigerator and wrote her name and number in red ink across it.

"Yes," Porter replied weakly. It was obvious that no other answer would be accepted. Elaine nodded and smiled. "I'll let you out."

At the door, Elaine stopped suddenly and turned, giving Porter an unexpected and very passionate kiss that left her breathless and off-balance. "I'll be seeing you, Porter." She was gone, and Porter closed the door behind her with an explosive sigh. Every nerve in her body jangled with sexual awareness, and she knew that when she moved she would feel wetness between her legs.

She had never felt this way for a woman. It had been almost six months since Beth's somewhat hasty departure, but even that period of celibacy could hardly account for the burning lusting hunger that the thought of Elaine Jessup's body engendered.

Growling to herself, Porter pushed off from the doorway and strode into the kitchen to have one last cup of coffee before heading to work.

Chapter IV.

"Uh oh." Porter looked up from her paperwork as her partner made another, less polite, comment.

"What's wrong?" Without another word, Joe handed her the file he was looking at. Glancing at it, Porter saw it was the toxicology report on Luke Williams' allergy medicine vial. She scanned through the technical wording, stopping dead at the analysis. "Shit."

"Tubocurarine chloride. Poison." Joe shook his head. "So much for accidental death."

"Curare. How the hell did someone get hold of curare?"

"Damned if I know." Porter turned her attention back to the report, reading it more carefully. There was hardly any allergy medicine in the vial at all. Someone had made very sure Luke Williams would drop dead as soon as he gave himself an injection.

"Any guesses on our prime suspect?"

"The bereaved widow would top my list," Joe said.

"Motive? Opportunity?"

Joe shrugged. "The opportunity is obvious. Motive? I haven't a clue. Maybe he was cheating on her."

"That's hardly a motive these days. We'd better move carefully."

Before Joe could answer, the lieutenant popped his head out of his office. "Sienna, Graves, get in here!"

"Oh, Christ," Porter muttered as she got up. "The shit's going to hit the fan now."

Lieutenant Day closed the door behind the two detectives and motioned them to chairs in front of his desk. He took his own seat and templed his fingers, looking them over.

"I've heard the Williams case is now a homicide."

"That's right. We just got the toxicology report back." Porter shifted uneasily. She and Lieutenant Day hadn't gotten along too well since she out shot him at last quarter's qualifying. He hated being beaten, and being beaten by a woman was even worse.

"You realize just how hot this case is going to get," Day said. "I've already heard from the mayor. I want this thing done right, do you understand me? Luke Williams was very influential in this town."

"We always do it the best we can," Joe said defensively.

"I'm glad you're on it, Sienna." He wouldn't call her by her first name. Never had. "Your background will be helpful."

"I haven't hung out with that set in years," Porter replied a little stiffly, wishing she could develop some sudden illness and be excused. The last thing she wanted was to have to poke around the lives of people at the club.

"Nevertheless. I want daily reports. And don't say anything to the press. Do you have any leads?"

"Not yet," Joe said. "But we have a list of witnesses to start with."

"Good. I expect kid gloves with these people, do I make myself clear?" *Perfectly clear*, Porter thought with a grimace. *Ignore anything untoward unless it pertains directly to the case.* She nodded. "That's all, then."

Back at her desk, Porter reached in a drawer and pulled out the phone book. "Mrs. Williams said her husband had his own investment company. That'd be a good place to start, don't you think?" She flipped the book open to the yellow pages and found the investments section. Williams Investments had a quarter page ad.

"You handle that and I'll go talk to the lab people." Joe shuffled some papers. Porter nodded absently, then suddenly straightened in her chair, her eyes glued to the ad. It listed all the partners and brokers individually. Two names under Luke Williams was Elaine Jessup.

"Oh, fucking Christ," she whispered. She tried to

tear her gaze away from the name, to no avail. *Oh, Christ.* Elaine was listed as a senior partner. She had spent the night with one of Luke Williams' senior partners. A possible suspect. Visions of trying to explain that conflict of interest swam in front of her eyes, making her feel slightly ill.

"Porter? You okay?" Joe's voice was concerned. "What's wrong?"

"Nothing. I - nothing. I'll handle Williams Investments." She stood abruptly and grabbed her blazer. *What the hell am I going to say to Elaine?* What could she say?

Driving down Elm Street toward the address listed for the company was sheer torture. At every light, Porter fought the urge to turn and go home, go anywhere but to that office. But at last she turned into the parking lot, saw the familiar silver Jaguar, and knew there was no other option but to face Elaine as a detective.

Pushing all thoughts of the previous night from her mind, Porter got out of her car and locked it, then turned and marched herself inside the building.

The layout was familiar, a receptionist desk blocking the way into a large open room from which opened private offices. A block of cubicles took up the center of the room, and an electronic ticker tape ran across one wall. The furniture was real wood, the plants obviously alive, everything exuding an air of success and wealth.

"May I help you?" The receptionist, unidentifiable from a million other receptionists, looked up at her questioningly from her seat of authority, waiting to see if Porter were to be allowed past.

Porter showed her badge and gave her name, then added, "Is Ms. Jessup in?"

"Ms. Jessup isn't available at this time - "

"I didn't ask if she was available." Porter startled herself with the fierceness in her voice. "I asked if she was in."

Looking shaken, the receptionist nodded. "But she's with a customer...."

Remembering her manners, and proper procedure, Porter took a deep breath. "How about Mr. Kyle?" Daniel Kyle had been listed as the other senior partner.

"Mr. Kyle is on vacation until the end of the week."

"Then I'll wait for Ms. Jessup." The receptionist looked relieved that proper form was to be followed.

"I'll let her know you're here. Would you like a cup of coffee?" Porter accepted and sat down in one of the leather easy chairs in the waiting area. No sooner had she received her coffee than Elaine came to the desk, a broad smile on her face.

"Detective! What a pleasure. Please, come into my office. Frances, hold my calls." Porter stood and followed Elaine back to a large oak-paneled office, fighting images of their lovemaking, of Elaine's lips and fingers hot on her body....

The door closed behind them, Elaine took a seat behind her immense desk and motioned for Porter to sit. "Well, Porter, this is a surprise. How did you find out where I work?"

"I didn't come here to see you." Not exactly true, but the truth might not come out right. Elaine frowned. "You don't know?"

"Know what?" Porter studied her. She seemed to be telling the truth.

"Luke Williams was murdered yesterday." Her statement was rewarded with the sight of Elaine going blank, then white, her jaw dropping open in shock. "At the club."

"Oh, my God. That's why he wasn't in this morning."

"Correct." Porter paused, then leaned forward. She caught a whiff of Elaine's perfume and felt momentarily dizzy. "I almost had a coronary when I saw your name associated with his."

"I'm not – I'm not a suspect, am I?"

"Honestly? I don't know. Should you be?" Looking Elaine in the eye, Porter asked again what she had asked facetiously the day before. This time she wasn't being funny. "Have you ever stolen, bribed, or otherwise screwed anybody?"

Elaine was silent for a moment, studying her. Then she swiveled in her chair and stood up, smoothing her business suit. "Come with me." Porter followed her into a slightly larger office. The large brass nameplate read Luke Williams. "I've been worried about something for a while now, and I think you should know about it."

"What's that?" Elaine pulled several files out of a drawer and spread them across the desk.

"There's something wrong with these accounts. Stocks double billed, margin charges wrong, transactions that don't exist. I'm not talking about minor figures, either."

Porter looked at her. "Embezzlement?"

"About two million dollars worth. And that's just in the last four or five months. I haven't been able to go back any farther." Porter recalled that Luke Williams had just paid cash for two brand new Mercedes convertibles. She looked again at the accounts.

"I need the names. Whose accounts are these?"

"Luke manages all the really big accounts. I have a list in my office of names. I wasn't sure who to turn to with this. To be honest, I was thinking of calling you about it today. If you'll notice, the skimming has been getting more and more obvious."

"How about his own account? Was he ahead or behind?" Elaine bent and typed in a password on the computer terminal sitting prominently on the desk, then a number. She studied the figures and frowned.

"He's taken some heavy losses. We all have, with the market being so unpredictable. But Luke was always a speculator. Took big chances on risky investments. He was right enough of the time to get a reputation." She looked up at Porter, her eyes expressive. "I had no idea he was dead. I wouldn't have asked you out if I'd known it was him."

"I am open to charges of conflict of interest," Porter responded somewhat dryly. "Not a position I enjoy being in, especially under the circumstances."

"I had no idea," she repeated.

"You told me you were in investments. You didn't mention you were a senior partner at a highly successful firm."

"I don't think you would have let me make love with you if I had." Porter shrugged; she was probably right. Elaine looked away. "How did he...."

"I can't say. If you need a warrant for those names, I'll be glad to get one."

"That isn't necessary. But I don't think you're going to like who's on it." They returned to Elaine's office. She handed Porter a single typewritten page with eight names and addresses on it, including those of the three men Williams had golfed with just prior to his death. And Blaine Sienna. Porter saw her father's name and drew in a sharp breath.

"Shit."

"I told you." Porter stared at her. "The other men are all close friends of Luke's. He must have been desperate to steal from them."

"Can you prove where you were yesterday, all day?"

Elaine frowned. "Well, yes, I can."

"Good." Porter managed a smile. "Not that I think it will be necessary for you to do so. It just makes me feel better." She paused, and thought for a moment. "Have you met Mrs. Williams?"

"Virginia? Of course. She's a little remote, but then so are most of the wives. Being out has its disadvantages."

"So you're out here? There's no chance at blackmail?"

"No. I came out as soon as my father died. I would have before that, but he had a bad heart, and I didn't want to be responsible for another heart attack."

"I see." Porter could also see the question in Elaine's eyes, and answered it before it could be put into words. "It's much different for me. My life is on the line every day."

"I understand." Elaine's voice was soft. "I can keep my mouth shut."

"I know." And Porter realized she had known. Had known from the first. Elaine might be open about herself, but she also had respect for others; a respect that Beth had lacked. Beth had come damn close to bringing Porter out during their breakup. Instinctively, Porter knew Elaine would never resort to such low tactics.

Jesus, even in the middle of a murder investigation this woman is getting to me! Porter didn't know what to make of her situation. Elaine was still a possible suspect, and here she was thinking about how the woman would act in a relationship. Porter shook her head and wondered if she needed a vacation.

A cigarette would be nice.... "Do you smoke?" Elaine had not the night before, but there hadn't been much opportunity. Smiling, Elaine shook her head, then opened a wooden box on her desk and offered it to her. Inside were cigarettes and a lighter.

Giving in, Porter took one and lit it. Inhaling deeply, watching the smoke curl up from the end, she mentally cursed herself for her weakness. It was the fourth time she had tried without success to quit. At least this time she'd made it more than a month.

"I understand how hard it can be," Elaine said, laughing. "I quit about two years ago. I just keep these around for customers."

"I quit when Beth left. Christ, it's been over six months now. She hated my smoking. Sometimes I think I did it just to annoy her."

Elaine raised an eyebrow at her. "I'll remember that."

Porter finished the cigarette. "I'll need a written statement from you about the embezzlement."

"I'll get on it right away." Elaine gave her a half-salute. "Don't work too hard, detective."

Standing, Porter grinned. "I wish it were that easy." She was at the door before Elaine spoke again, sounding almost shy this time.

"Porter - feel free to call me any time. Even if you

just want to talk."

Porter studied her and felt a surge of an emotion she had thought extinct in her heart. "I will."

* * * * *

On the way back to the station, Porter stopped and bought a pack of cigarettes and a lighter. Feeling only slightly annoyed with her weakness, she made her way to the detectives' room and to her desk. Joe was sitting at his studying a file.

"How'd it go?"

"Wonderful," Porter replied in a sarcastic tone. "I got more work for us." She flipped the paper at him and watched his face. He grimaced.

"Who are these people?"

"According to a source at Williams' office, people he was embezzling money from."

"Christ. This Blaine fellow - he related to you?"

"He's my father." Joe looked up at her in surprise. Porter hadn't talked about her family much, with reason. Yesterday had been the first time she had seen her father in almost two years.

"Is it - do you want me to take him?"

"No. You take these four, I'll handle the others." She pointed to the four strange names. She would be more effective with the ones who knew her already. Joe nodded, understanding her thinking.

"After lunch?"

"I think we should talk to Virginia Williams again. This embezzlement angle throws a different light on the case. I want to see what she knows about it."

Joe stood and reached for his jacket. "Might as well get it out of the way now." On the way to the car, he looked over at her as she lit a cigarette. "I thought you quit."

"I did." He lapsed into silence. Porter savored the taste of the tobacco as she tried to steel herself for the scene she knew would be awaiting them at the Williams' house.

They rode in different cars, and the drive gave Porter time to think about Elaine, although she would have preferred not to. There was something special about Elaine, something different. All of Porter's previous lovers had been from out of town, from different backgrounds. Beth was the daughter of a South Carolina farmer and had only completed high school and a nursing assistant course. Before her had been Cindy, a teacher's aide, and before that Martha. Martha hadn't done much of anything, as far as Porter remembered.

She had always been the butch, the breadwinner. Before she had become a police officer, she had worked for her father as a stock analyst. If not for their falling out, she might have been sitting in an office like Elaine's. Even after seven years, she had known exactly what the figures on the account sheets meant, had even recognized a few of the stock symbols.

Elaine had an MBA; Porter had seen the diploma on her wall. She probably pulled in a couple hundred thousand a year. She was educated and intelligent, and damn good in bed. She scared the hell out of Porter.

And yet, that very fear made her attractive. Like a moth to a flame, Porter felt herself being pulled into Elaine's light, and it confused her that she was putting up so little struggle.

Chapter V.

The scene at the Williams' house could only be described as pandemonium. Cars lined both sides of the street for a block in either direction. Porter groaned to herself, even though she had been expecting something like this. She remembered her own mother's death, and the mob scene following that.

Parking her car in a space just vacated by a Rolls-Royce, Porter got out and looked for Joe; she spotted him walking down the street toward her, one hand in his pocket, trying to look casual. She should have warned him. A small grin crossed her face. Maybe not.

"Who are all these people?" He asked when he drew abreast of her.

"Well-wishers. Come on, let's get this over with." She led the way up the drive and to the front door, which stood open, only a glass storm door blocking their way. Porter pulled the door open and stepped inside, catching Joe's startled look out of the corner of her eye. How could she explain that the door was open because people were expected to walk in?

There was a guest register open on the table in the hall, and Porter glanced at it curiously. She recognized several of the names on that page alone. "Porter!"

Jumping, Porter looked up to see her aunt standing next to her, holding a Jell-O mold. "Aunt Fay! I didn't know you knew the Williams."

"Virginia is in my bridge club. What are you doing here?"

"Official business, I'm afraid. Is Mrs. Williams here?" She caught another look on Joe's face, a look that asked why the door would be open if she wasn't, and shot one back at him to keep his mouth closed. He was out of his league.

"Yes, she's in the den. You look good, dear."

"Thank you, aunt Fay. Where's the den?" With her aunt leading the way, and fighting a feeling that she was sixteen again, Porter walked through the living room and dining room and into the kitchen, passing people she knew right and left. Keeping her gaze directly ahead, she prayed she wouldn't be stopped.

Fay motioned toward a door at the far end of the kitchen. "The den's through there." Porter nodded and started toward the door. Joe touched her arm as they neared.

"Do you want to handle this?" He seemed uncomfortable. Porter shook her head.

"We both ought to be there in case she says something important."

Virginia Williams was sitting on a sofa, wearing a black dress and hat. She was surrounded by what appeared to be her family. A few people, women mostly, stood in a loose queue waiting to talk to her.

The queen and her entourage holding court, Porter thought. Virginia looked up and saw her and went pale. Her hand went to her throat, to the same strand of pearls she had worn the day before. Porter forced herself to be impassive and official as she stepped to the head of the line.

"Mrs. Williams, would it be possible to have a few minutes of your time?"

"Of course." She rose. A young man bearing a strong resemblance to Luke Williams, put a hand out.

"Mother, who are these people?" She turned and gave him a withering look, and he subsided, staring at the floor.

"Please, come with me." She led the way through another long hall and into a small sitting room. "Have you any news? I was shocked to hear that Luke had been murdered."

Porter and Joe exchanged looks. "How did you find that out, Mrs. Williams," Joe asked.

"Why, I called the police department and some nice young man told me." Porter cursed inwardly. She'd find out who that nice young man was and discipline him for giving out information over the phone.

"The reason we came over, Mrs. Williams," Porter began, "was that we have come into some evidence that your husband was embezzling funds from his customers' stock accounts."

The first expression to cross the woman's face was rage. That was quickly replaced by a studied blankness. "Who told you that?"

"One of the senior partners." Porter wouldn't bring up Elaine's name unless forced to. Virginia considered a scant moment, then shook her head ruefully.

"What will she think of next?"

"I beg your pardon?" Joe perked up. "What will who think of next?"

"Elaine Jessup. Why, she was here just yesterday evening, threatening to expose this so-called embezzlement unless I made certain arrangements with regard to the company. I think she had been making the same threats to poor Luke."

"Why didn't you mention this yesterday, about your husband, I mean?" Joe had his notepad open, his pen busy.

"I was distraught. I couldn't think straight. But then, after that woman had the nerve to show up here ... I wouldn't be surprised if she was the one who poisoned Luke."

Porter's mind spun. She forced herself to concentrate even as she heard her own voice. "What time did she arrive?"

"Oh, it was almost eight o'clock. I believe she had been drinking. I wasn't surprised, you know. Luke told me she was one of those women. He would have fired her if her father hadn't been such a dear friend." Porter's thoughts clicked into sudden coherence. Virginia Williams was lying. Elaine couldn't possibly have been at Virginia's house at eight. At eight o'clock last night, Elaine Jessup had been in Porter's apartment, with her face buried between Porter's thighs. But she couldn't possibly call Virginia on the lie, not without revealing how she knew it to be a lie.

"What makes you think the embezzlement was a fraud?"

"Oh, I didn't say that. I just think it far more likely that someone who would try to blackmail a widow, one of those kind of women, would embezzle funds than a successful man like my husband."

"What do you mean by one of those women, Mrs. Williams?" Porter forced her voice to remain level. Virginia Williams turned a look on her that made her cringe.

"Why, a lesbian, of course."

"Being lesbian hardly predisposes someone to committing a crime," Joe commented, startling Porter.

"So you say. But she was still here making threats."

"I see." Porter stood, unwilling to remain in the room with this lying, self-centered woman one second longer. Any sympathy, any liking she had felt for her had vanished the moment she had besmeared Elaine's name. "Thank you for your time, Mrs. Williams."

"Of course. I do hope you establish some solid leads soon, Detective."

"Thank you," Joe responded. Porter couldn't help but notice the stiffness in his voice, and wondered if it were a response to her own sudden coldness. Mrs. Williams pointed the way out before returning to the den, and the two detectives let themselves out.

Outside, Porter blew out her breath in an angry rush. She couldn't afford to let a one night stand skew her thinking in a case a touchy as this one, and yet all she could think about was protecting Elaine's name. Joe looked curiously at her. "Looks like we should investigate this Elaine Jessup woman," he said.

"Virginia Williams was lying."

"How do you know that? If the Jessup woman was making threats, it makes her a definite possible."

They were by Porter's car. She studied Joe for a long, silent while, judging how she should proceed. She didn't want to cause a scene out here in the open, but if she allowed Joe to write anything official about what Virginia had said, she would either have to lie herself or make what she knew she should say official as well.

"Joe, I just know."

"That isn't good enough, Porter." He wasn't being difficult, but he knew the procedures as well as she did. Just knowing something was never good enough.

Porter sighed. "Elaine Jessup is the blonde you saw yesterday. She was at my place last night at eight."

"Maybe Mrs. Williams had the time wrong." Joe pursed his lips and looked back at her. Porter sighed again. In for a dime, in for a dollar....

"Elaine came over before six. She left at six thirty this morning."

"Oh." Joe raised an eyebrow and looked away for a moment. When his gaze returned to her, it was unexpectedly soft. "I already knew you were, Porter."

"Christ. Who else knows? The whole god damned department?"

"No. Just me. I don't give a shit, personally. I got a cousin who's gay. But this could cause a problem. Why do you think she lied?"

Porter looked at Joe in a new light. "Either she's protecting her husband or herself. I don't know. But there must be some way to prove she's a liar without me having to announce to the world that I spent the night with the woman she's accusing."

"I don't know, Porter. I just don't know. She couldn't have snuck out...."

"Joe, I can guarantee you that Elaine Jessup was far too busy between seven and about eleven to even think about sneaking out of my apartment. Besides, I live twenty minutes from here, I'm fairly certain I'd have noticed if she was gone for an hour."

"You realize the potential for conflict of interest here, don't you?" Joe shifted from one foot to the other. "Why her? Why last night?"

"I didn't know who she worked for until this morning. And last night ... it's been over six months, Joe." He stared at her. "Yeah, I know, it blows the image of us nympho lesbians and our non-stop one night stands out the window, doesn't it."

"Six months - Jesus, I'd go nuts!" He seemed to realize suddenly that they were standing in the road discussing their sex lives and turned red. "Look, let's get on with these interviews. Maybe by the time we get back to the office one of us will have come up with a solution to your problem."

"Okay. Hey, Joe." Joe had started to walk away and turned back around when she called. Porter smiled at him. "You're all right."

"Yeah, so are you, Porter." She watched him walk up the hill toward his car and was once again amazed at the people who unexpectedly accepted her for who she was. Her aunt Fay was another.

As she started her car and started toward her father's house, she remembered when she finally decided to break the news to her aunt. Fay had been like a mother to her, and it seemed only right that Porter turn to her when she had decided to stop hiding from her father.

* * * * *

"Aunt Fay - I need to talk to you." Porter had been

- 66 -

sitting on the back porch with Fay for an hour, making conversation as she tried to work up her nerve. Fay looked at her over her iced tea.

"Well, it's important - no, I guess it isn't important, except to me." She felt foolish. She was in love with Cindy, she knew it. And her decision to stop working for her father had been made. But the words were still so difficult. Even at twenty-seven, even having been a lesbian all her life, the words were still difficult.

"You're babbling, dear."

"I know. Aunt Fay, there's this woman, and ... well, we ... I...."

Fay waited.

"I'm a lesbian."

Fay raised an eyebrow. "And?" she prompted. "What's your point?"

"Did you hear me? I said I was a lesbian."

Fay sighed and put down her drink. She studied her fingernails for a long moment. "Porter, when you were thirteen, your mother bemoaned to me that you didn't seem the slightest bit interested in boys. I told her to give it some time. When you were fifteen I told her to be happy you weren't out having sex. When you were seventeen, well, there wasn't any point. She knew as well as I did why you weren't dating."

"She never said anything to me about it ...."

"She didn't have the words."

Porter considered for a moment. "What about - Dad?"

- 67 -

"Your father is a different matter entirely."

"He doesn't know?" Porter felt her spirit sink.

"Oh, I'm sure he suspects. But he doesn't want to know."

"How about you? How do you feel about it?" Porter held her breath and waited for her aunt's response. Fay considered her question.

"I accept you for you, Porter. There's enough sadness in this world as it is, without wishing it on someone." Then she picked up her tea and changed the subject as if they had been discussing the weather or something else equally unimportant.

*   *   *   *   *

Porter's father had not taken the news quite so well. It was, Porter thought now, one of the big mistakes in her life, forcing him to face the truth of his daughter's lesbianism. If she hadn't gotten angry with him, hadn't hurled it in his face in spite, perhaps things might have turned out differently.

But she was young and filled with a lot of misplaced idealism then, idealism that said the world would have to accept you if you made sure they knew who you were. And when she had decided to become a police officer, she had been so afraid suddenly that her father would tell that she had withdrawn from him.

Yes, looking back she could see where she was

equally to blame for the division between them. But it had been too long to attempt a reconciliation now. She would just interview him and be done with it, and hopefully he wouldn't say anything to make himself a suspect. If he did, she would have no choice but to bow out of the case. She might be able to justify staying on if Elaine were a suspect, but not her father.

As she drove, something nagged her about Virginia Williams' comments. Something beyond irritation at her lying and her attitude toward lesbians. But for some reason, she couldn't put her finger on it. Annoyed, Porter stepped on the gas and sped down the next two blocks. She couldn't let her own personal feelings affect her judgment. If she started doing that, she might as well turn in her badge and go back to stock analysis.

Crossing Cornwallis, Porter came to a stop at the next street down, Kimberly, then turned right. Two blocks later, she slowed down. With a deep sigh and a mental reminder to keep calm, she parked in front of the house in which she had spent her youth.

Chapter VI.

Firming her resolve, Porter walked up the front steps and pressed the doorbell. A minute later, the large white wood door opened to reveal her father's second wife. Porter groaned inwardly even as she forced a smile to her face.

"Hello, Susan. Is my father home?"

Susan stared at her for a moment. "Yes, he is. Won't you come in?" She stepped back to allow Porter to cross the threshold. The house looked remarkably unchanged, even after all the years. The only thing foreign was Susan. Porter quickly turned her mind from that course of thought.

"I need to speak with him." Susan went over to the stairs and yelled up them for her husband, then returned to the entry where Porter still stood.

"Come into the study." In the small room which separated the entry hall from the den, Porter chose an armchair, leaving her father the sofa. "Would you like something to drink? Tea? A Coke perhaps?"

Even though she wasn't supposed to drink on duty, Porter couldn't resist reminding Susan that she was hardly a teenager any more. "I'd like a bourbon and water, please."

Looking a little startled, which was the desired effect, Susan turned and opened the closet into which the bar had been built and fixed the drink. Porter had a chance to take a sip before her father appeared in the doorway.

"What do you want?" His tone was gruff. Porter sat her glass down and pulled out her notepad.

"You told me I should stop by, remember?"

"You could have called," he responded, crossing his arms. Porter counted to ten and forced her tone to be pleasant.

"I'm here on official business, father. Please sit down."

"I'd rather stand, thank you. What sort of official business? Does this have anything to do with that mess at the club yesterday?" Porter smothered a grin. Her father hadn't changed much; he still wanted to be the one asking all the questions.

"I'm investigating the death of Luke Williams. I understand you had an account with Williams Investments."

"Yes, I did. Luke was a friend of mine."

Porter studied his face intently while she made the next statement. "We have uncovered evidence that Mr. Williams was embezzling funds from client accounts. Including yours."

Blaine Sienna's face turned white, then red, then started to tinge with purple. "That bastard!"

"So I take it you were unaware of Mr. Williams' activities?" Porter made a note on her pad.

"Completely. That son of a bitch."

Porter looked up at him and weighed her next words carefully. "I find it hard to believe that you wouldn't notice errors in your account, considering you yourself used to be in investments."

"I trusted him. The figures always looked right." He looked at her with new eyes. "Someone killed him, didn't they."

"It appears that Mr. Williams may have met with foul play, yes," Porter responded quietly. "We are still investigating."

"Damn it, Porter, I don't know anything about it."

"You don't know of anyone who would have a reason to kill him?"

He stared at her again. "Well, obviously if someone found out he was stealing money - but even then I can't imagine someone from the club killing over something like that."

"Well, he did die in the club house."

"Have you considered the idea that someone came in and killed him? It must have been an outsider. You know, of course, that no one in our group would do anything so base as to kill someone." His sincerity in something so ridiculous would have been amusing had it not been so real.

"So you think the club society is above murder? Really, Father, I would think you had better sense than that. Or have you forgotten the Travis case already?" Mr. John Travis, a noted local textile manufacturer, had come home to his expensive lakeside home with a pistol and shot his wife and four children. Only the youngest girl, a child of three, had lived.

"John Travis was deranged. It was one incident. It must have been an outsider, you see that, don't you?"

"I see." Porter was secretly relieved that he hadn't fallen apart and started blaming everyone he could think of. But she detected his not so subtle attempt at influencing her away from considering anyone who would have actually had a reason to commit murder. She closed her notebook. "Then I won't take up any more of your time."

Her father was still blocking the doorway, his face stern. Porter knew instinctively she was about to get a lecture, and tried to gird herself not to respond.

"You still think playing cop is better than working for me, I take it?" A new tactic, his tone was almost conversational. Porter refused to be fooled.

"I don't want to have an argument with you." She stood up.

"You could be making a hundred grand a year by now. Instead you're getting what, maybe eighteen thousand? You don't belong there, Porter. You were born above all that."

Porter counted to ten. "I made my career choice carefully. I happen to enjoy what I do. It brings me satisfaction."

"Like screwing around with those women does? What's this one's name, Beth?" Even though their parting had been under less than friendly circumstances, Porter bristled at the way her father spoke Beth's name.

"Beth left six months ago. And my love life is not any of your concern."

"You certainly thought it was when you threw it in my face!" Her father was building a good head of steam, but Porter didn't care. She was getting too angry.

"That was seven years ago. I've changed a great deal since then."

"Changed – hah! You still think you're some strange kind of pseudo-man. You're thirty-four years old, Porter. You should be married by now, have children, for god's sake!"

"If I wanted children I would have children, Father. I have a career."

"All of your old friends have married." He drove the point home by jabbing his finger at her. "I've sent baby presents to half a dozen this year."

"And most of them have been divorced at least once," Porter spat in return. "Why would I want to let myself be trapped into this twisted curse you call a life when I can be myself?"

"At least their relationships have been sanctified by the church."

"If I could have married Beth I would have." This was getting away from her, and fast. She drew in a deep breath and forced it out slowly. "I would rather be happy some of the time than miserably married all of the time."

"I don't understand where we went wrong with you, Porter, I honestly don't. How you can repay everything we've done for you with this ...." Porter felt her anger peaking and knew it was time to go.

"I appreciate everything you've done for me, Father." She made certain her voice contained no hint of sarcasm. "I don't see how you can be unhappy with having an adult child who makes her own decisions."

"When those decisions are so against everything I believe in?" Blaine Sienna planted his fists on his waist. Porter sighed. *It's the same damn fight, seven years later and the same damn fight.*

"I'm leaving. If I need a statement, my partner will come get it from you. See you in another two years."

Her father didn't answer. Grinding her teeth, Porter stormed out of the house and to her car, slamming the car door behind her. She sat there for a minute, shaking with anger, then lit a cigarette. A few deep breaths and she was calm enough to drive.

Putting the car into gear, she slipped away from the curb and headed downtown. Time for lunch and a break.

*   *   *   *   *

After lunch, Porter went to Frank Simms' automotive dealership. She ignored the twinge of jealousy she felt when she saw the rows of shiny new Mercedes, Jaguars, and Land Rovers, and strode into the showroom to ask for Mr. Simms.

He was as enthusiastic as before as he came out to greet her with a hearty handshake. He made jokes the entire way to his office, but when the door closed, he sank into his chair and put his arms on the desk.

"I heard someone did old Williams in. Is that true?"

"Who told you that?" Porter was startled once again.

"Virginia. Poor girl, she's heartbroken over this. He's finally gotten away from her. She was always after him to do something or other."

"Mrs. Williams was domineering?"

"Oh, yes. When Luke came in to buy those cars I told you about, he went on and on about how Virginia just insisted they get new models. He had just bought new cars last year, but she always wanted the newest, the best."

Porter digested this bit of information and considered. "I understand you had an account with

Mr. Williams' investment company."

"Well, yes I did." Frank Simms frowned. "Why?"

"Were you aware that he was embezzling funds from his accounts?"

Frank's reaction was very similar to Blaine Sienna's, except in his case the transformation was even more startling. "What?"

"Mr. Williams took funds from several accounts, including yours. The total amount was rather large." Porter looked for signs of guilt. There were none, only disbelief and shock.

"I don't believe it. I just ... I can't believe it. Luke would never do something like that."

"Did Mr. Williams gamble?"

"Not to my knowledge. We often bet on the course, but Luke never took part. He said gambling was something a man who worked with money should avoid."

Porter made a note. "So he struck you as being careful with money?"

"Scrupulously careful. Now, Virginia is a different story. She likes to keep up with the Joneses, if you know what I mean."

"Do you think she was capable of killing to do so?" Frank's laugh was instantaneous and hearty.

"Virginia? No. She's just a housewife. A pampered, rich housewife, but a housewife. I doubt she could conceive of a plot to kill her husband, much less carry it out."

Porter made a note. "Anything else you can tell me about Mr. Williams that might give us a motive to why someone would kill him? An affair, perhaps?"

"Luke Williams was unswervingly devoted to Virginia. He would have had to be, to stay with her for so long. If anyone was going to kill anyone, I would have thought he would kill her, just to be rid of her."

"Why do you say that?" Porter looked up at him and raised an eyebrow. Frank shrugged.

"I grew up in the club, but I'm not one of the richest members. I made my money myself, here. My wife is thankfully satisfied with what I make, because she remembers when we didn't have nearly so much. Virginia was an Armstrong. She expected a certain level of wealth from the start. I think Luke's bad heart came from working himself half to death trying to make enough money to please her."

"Mr. Williams had children, didn't he?" Frank Simms seemed to be an unexpectedly rich fount of information all of a sudden.

"Oh, yes, a boy and a girl. Their mother has both them under her thumb. Luke Jr. won't hardly piss without her permission - oh, excuse me, detective. I forgot I was speaking to a lady."

Porter laughed shortly. "I hear worse every day, Mr. Simms." She made notes, then on a whim asked, "Do you know Elaine Jessup?"

"Well, yes. She's a senior partner of Luke's. She

buys her cars from me. A nice woman, although I can't see why she insists on flouting her sexuality around."

"What was her relationship with Mr. Williams like?"

Simms shifted uneasily, and Porter's attention focused more sharply on him. He lifted his hands in a gesture of futility, then dropped them again. "I suppose you need to know everything, and I doubt anyone else will tell you this. Elaine had an affair with Luke's daughter Michelle, a few years ago. Michelle's twenty-five or six now, lives in Raleigh. Virginia was fit to be tied about it."

"And Mr. Williams?"

Frank leaned forward. "Let me tell you something. Even if Luke Williams did steal money from me, I still think he was possibly the most caring father in Hanes Park. He'd have done anything for his children. When Virginia told him to fire Elaine, he flat refused. Michelle left Elaine, if I remember correctly, and Luke felt bad about it."

"So their relationship was a good one?" Porter tried to keep her voice level. Michelle Williams was another lesbian from Hanes Park; there were turning out to be quite a few.

"They tolerated each other. Luke thought Elaine was too old to be with Michelle, but she made her happy for a while, so he didn't press the issue. Virginia hated her. Still does."

"So Ms. Jessup had no reason to kill Mr. Williams?"

Frank laughed again and shook his head. "Hardly. Thanks to him she was able to buy two new cars this year."

"She didn't pay cash, did she?"

"She might have. It happens. She bought a Jaguar about four months ago and a Land Rover about nine. Her father was a friend of mine ... speaking of which, you look very familiar. Are you any relation to Blaine Sienna?"

Porter blushed. "Yes. He's my father." She stood up. "Thank you for your time, Mr. Simms. I'll need you to sign a statement about what you've told me."

Frank Simms stood as well. "Of course, anything to help the police. You people did a good job stopping the vandalism problem I had last year. By the way, I noticed you drive a Saturn. A good car, but if you decide to trade up, please stop by. I'm sure we can work out a good deal for Blaine's daughter."

"Thank you, Mr. Simms." She shook his hand and left the office. She couldn't afford any of the cars he sold, although a Land Rover would be nice. She was too busy saving her money for a house, though. A nice, small brick house with a fenced back yard and a deck big enough for a hot tub. She was tired of living in apartments.

In the car, she glanced down at her list. Dr. Archibald was the next closest address. She didn't expect to gain much by talking to him, but Elaine had said all of the names on the list were close friends of Luke's. John Archibald had not indicated that during their initial conversation. Porter wondered if perhaps he had learned something that caused him to stop considering Luke a close friend.

*   *   *   *   *

Dr. John Archibald's office was in a trendy medical center off Wendover, ironically the same center where Porter's orthodontist, Dr. Weaver, had worked. As she pulled into the parking lot, her teeth started a dull ache. *Ah, memories....*

After showing her badge to two different secretaries, she was shown into Dr. Archibald's office, not as large as Elaine's, with white walls and functional furniture. The only truly personal item Porter could see was a large framed photograph of the doctor with his family, the blue of the ocean in the background. The doctor himself joined her a few minutes later, removing the white dental tunic that covered his dress shirt as he came in. "What can I do for you, Detective?"

"I have a few more questions about Mr. Williams." She repeated her spiel about the embezzlement, was met with a similar shock and anger, and a denial of any knowledge about it.

"Do you know Virginia Williams?" She noticed that he hesitated, glanced away from her for a moment.

"Not well. My wife went to college with her, but they don't associate much."

Porter asked a few more questions, trying to double check what Frank Simms had told her. John Archibald confirmed a few statements, but didn't seem to know, or be willing to discuss, as much about Luke Williams as Frank had. Porter decided to change tactics.

"I was told you were a close friend of Mr. Williams. You don't seem to share that opinion. Why is that?"

John Archibald stared at her as if she had just sprouted horns. "He was a friend, that's all. We played golf together. Once in a while I'd go to watch a football game at his house. I don't know who told you we were close, but they were wrong. Luke didn't have many close friends; I don't think his wife liked to share him."

Porter made some notes, then looked around the office and tried to sound casual as she asked, "Do you know of a drug named tubocurarine chloride?"

"Of course, it's used in anesthesia. I don't use it here, though. I don't have the facilities for ventilating patients and I don't need it. I believe it's used mostly in lung surgery."

"Could you get hold of it?" John looked down his long nose at her.

"Are you implying that I might have?" His voice was stiff.

"No, sir. I am merely trying to determine how

easily the drug is available." Porter didn't want to alienate a witness, not without cause. "If it's purpose is so specific, it wouldn't be easy for someone not associated with the medical profession to obtain, would it?"

"No. I suppose I could order it from the pharmacy, but there would be a record made. Was that how Luke was killed?"

Porter swallowed. "It appears he was poisoned, yes."

"I'll be damned. You don't expect that to happen at the club, now do you?" The question was rhetorical, but Porter couldn't help but answer.

"I'd expect just about anything to happen at the club. It probably already has."

*   *   *   *   *

Later, driving back toward Elm Street, Porter thought over her first interview with Virginia Williams. She had just returned from the hospital when they arrived. Could she have gotten curare from someone there?

Deciding to put off the interview with Philip Weakly, Porter turned toward Irving Memorial Hospital. As she drove slowly along the winding, park-like front lawn of the hospital, she fought the panic that visits to the place always brought on. Her mother had died in the cancer wing of that hospital.

It took some time to find the pharmacy, but when she arrived, she was rewarded with a handsome looking woman with pecan skin and sparkling chestnut eyes who didn't need a pinky ring to identify her as a dyke. The short cut of her kinky black hair and pink diamond earrings gave her away.

Porter took a deep breath and allowed herself a moment to appreciate the woman's beauty, then pulled out her badge and introduced herself. The woman's nametag read 'Margaret Carey, DPh, Pharmacy'. Behind her, two younger men in lab coats scurried about.

"Dr. Carey, I need to ask you a few questions in regard to a case we're currently working on."

"Well, Ms. Sienna." The emphasis on the Ms. and a broad smile told Porter she wasn't hiding anything herself. "I'll be glad to help any way I can."

"Do you know a Virginia Williams?" There was a crash behind the counter and Porter caught a glimpse of the two men bending to collect bottles of pills that spilled from a dropped box.

"Oh, Mrs. Williams volunteers here. Has for centuries. I've seen her around."

"Has she ever visited with you?" The pharmacy door opened and one of the young men pushed a metal cart out into the hall. As he went past, he gave Porter a haughty, almost disgusted look, as if decrying that a dyke cop would be talking to his dyke supervisor.

"Well, she's brought magazines by, but no one's allowed into the pharmacy without authorization." Porter realized she was being appraised in a fairly frank manner. *Damn.*

"Do you keep records to prevent theft of drugs?" It was a stupid, but necessary question. Porter had to follow a slow and steady line of inquiry. Margaret laughed.

"Of course. Auditors would have our rear ends if we didn't. What are you getting at?"

"How hard would it be to check your records?" Porter was feeling a little warm under the liquid chocolate gaze. Margaret Carey wasn't tall, but she was muscular. *And good looking.*

"It's all right here," Margaret responded, patting the computer monitor next to her. "But I can't just start typing away, not without a release from administration. Hospital policy."

"Well," Porter decided to use what she had to her advantage and pulled out her card. "If you should happen to be typing away later and come across any missing tubocurarine chloride, or if you don't, give me a call."

Margaret accepted the card and smiled again, conspiratorially. "I see."

"I'll be back tomorrow to get a release for the information. Have a nice day." She left the counter and strolled back toward the entrance, wondering if she would ask Margaret Carey out given the chance. Quite possibly. That would give her father fits. Not only was he an intolerant homophobic asshole, he was also a bigot.

The day seemed much brighter as Porter got back into her car and headed toward Philip Weakly's office.

Chapter VII.

Philip Weakly yielded no new information, and within the hour Porter was back at the station, staring over a cup of coffee as Joe bent over his notes. Finally, he lifted his head and grimaced at her.

"Killing somebody over money. Crazy world, isn't it? It ain't like these people couldn't afford to lose a little cash."

"I'm not so sure that was the motive," Porter returned. "But for the life of me I can't puzzle out what the motive could be." She quickly filled Joe in on the results of her interviews. He sat back and thought about what she was saying.

"My guys said pretty much the same thing; Luke Williams was a hen-pecked husband who'd do anything for his wife. So why would she kill him? Seems to me she had things just the way she wanted them."

"Me too. I don't know, Joe, I'm brain fried." She stretched. "I need a shower and a good night's sleep."

"Are you going to be seeing...." Joe trailed off. "Never mind. I don't want to know."

Porter looked at him. "No, I'm not."

"I still haven't figured out what to do about her." He glanced at his notes. "I can't just omit Virginia Williams' accusation from my report."

"Give me until tomorrow," Porter said. "Let me think on it tonight. There must be some way to trap her in the lie without getting into where Elaine actually was." Joe nodded. Standing, Porter finished her coffee and pulled on her blazer. "See you later."

*   *   *   *   *

Porter's apartment seemed unusually empty when she let herself in. The two glasses she and Elaine had been drinking from still sat on the coffee table, and she automatically picked them up on the way past, smelling stale liquor. In the kitchen, she turned both upside down in the sink and left them there, then wandered into the bedroom to change.

Pulling her work clothes off, she took a shower and dressed in jeans and a sweatshirt, then returned to the kitchen and studied the contents of her refrigerator before deciding to order Chinese. Sitting at the table to wait for the delivery, she flipped through her mail and tried to ignore the silence. When it became too much, she went and turned on the stereo and replaced the CD with something more upbeat.

The Indigo Girls sang through the speakers, and Porter fixed herself a drink. She thought about Elaine. The bed was still unmade in the bedroom, the rumpled mess of the sheets a mute statement to what had happened the previous night.

After dinner, Porter gave in to an urge she had been fighting all evening. Picking up the phone, she dialed the number on the message board. It rang twice, then a woman picked up. "Elaine?"

"No. Hang on just a minute." Porter heard whomever it was yell for Elaine, and a minute later the familiar voice came over the receiver.

"Hello?"

"Elaine, this is Porter."

"Hi! I wasn't expecting you to call tonight. How are you?" Porter felt uncomfortable.

"I'm interrupting something. I shouldn't have called...."

"Nonsense."

"Then who answered the phone?" Who would answer the phone at someone else's house unless they felt they belonged there?

"Oh, that's just Toby."

Porter felt an unexpected pang of jealousy. "Who's Toby?"

"A friend." Elaine's voice was suddenly flat. "Why do you care?"

"Because - because...." *Because what?* What right did she have to demand to know who was there?

Porter bit her lip. The next words were unplanned. "Why didn't you tell me you'd had an affair with Michelle Williams?"

The pain in Elaine's voice was obvious. "Who told you about her?"

"That doesn't matter."

"I don't want to talk about Michelle. It was three years ago, it's over. I've gone on with my life." She sounded strained. Porter ground her teeth together as she pictured just how Elaine had gone on with her life; how many women did she sleep with?

"You do get around, don't you?" The words came out with more sharpness than Porter had intended and she cringed when she heard Elaine's sudden intake of breath.

"What the hell is that supposed to mean? You don't own me. After one night, you sure as hell don't own me."

"I'm putting my ass on the line for you, Elaine. Maybe I won't do that. Maybe I'll just let Joe handle you from now on. I don't think you'd like to be that involved in this," Porter snapped.

"I didn't ask you to protect me. I don't need protection, Porter. What the hell is wrong with you?"

"God damn it, Elaine...." Porter cut herself off. She forced a breath. "Goodbye." Slamming the phone down, she jerked out of her chair and stormed across the kitchen floor, then stopped and leaned against the doorframe, feeling drained.

What did Elaine mean to her? After one night of admittedly outstanding sex, she had no right to make any claims, didn't want to make any claims.

So much for a good night's sleep. Growling angrily, Porter stomped into the living room and retrieved her drink from where she had left it. Adding more bourbon to mask the taste of melted ice, she took a swallow and let the burn take away some of the anger, then lit a cigarette.

Filthy habit, she thought as she paced through the apartment. *A damn filthy habit.* She was still thinking it when she lit a second one ten minutes later.

So what if Elaine Jessup had a different woman for each night of the week? What damned difference did it make? They had enjoyed each other's company for an evening, that was all. No promises had been made, nor any expected. Porter paced and smoked and sipped at her drink. It had to be Beth.

Abruptly, the thought striking home like a pitcher's fast ball, Porter stopped. She was still reacting to Beth after all these months. Beth's infidelities still stung deeply. Porter sighed. She shouldn't have let her mouth get the better of her. Now Elaine would think she was some sort of possessive psycho bitch from hell, would never want to see her again.

Porter sank down onto the sofa and dropped her head. She really needed to learn to control her temper better. She stayed in that position for a long while, then forced herself to get up and pick out a book from her bookshelf. Going into the bedroom, she pulled off her clothes and climbed into bed.

Chapter VIII.

The next morning, instead of going directly into work, Porter went to the Williams house. It was early, and so there weren't any other visitors. Porter rang the front doorbell, which was answered by the young man she now guessed to be Luke Jr.

"May I help you?"

Porter showed him her badge. "I'd like to speak with your mother."

"Come in." He was a nervous sort, fidgeting with the handle of the door as she stepped into the foyer. "We're just through with breakfast." They went into the kitchen, where the Williams clan was gathered. Virginia sat at the head of the table, wearing another expensive looking black dress and the ever-present pearls. On her left sat a young woman in her mid-twenties, probably Michelle Williams.

"Mrs. Williams, I'm sorry to keep bothering you." Porter said, to put her at ease.

"Anything I can do to help your investigation, dear. Would you like some breakfast? Coffee?" Porter declined both. She would accept nothing from this woman. "Then shall we go into the den?"

"Yes." Once they were there, Virginia seated on a tufted leather sofa that was probably older than Porter and Porter herself standing, she dropped her civility a notch. "Something you said to me yesterday has been bothering me."

"What is that, dear?"

"Your accusations against Elaine Jessup." She noted the narrowing of Virginia's eyes, the way she glanced toward the kitchen door. "I know they were completely false."

"Why, whatever are you talking about?" She was acting and Porter knew it.

"I know you hate Elaine Jessup, and I know why. But that is no excuse for lying to a police officer." Virginia turned a faint shade of red.

"That woman corrupted my baby," she replied huffily. "Forced her into an unnatural relationship ..."

"I doubt that."

"Well, we were able to get her help, get her cured. But Elaine didn't want to let go. Said the most horrible things about us...."

Porter didn't want to let the conversation degenerate into a discussion of Virginia's feelings about Elaine. "What does that have to do with your husband's death?"

Virginia didn't appear to have heard her. "Why Luke didn't fire her, I'll never know. She must have threatened to expose her liaison with Michelle, used something to keep her position. I told him he'd be better off without her."

"Mrs. Williams, why did you lie to me?" Porter made her voice hard, official. Virginia looked at her helplessly. *As helpless as a tiger*, Porter thought viciously.

"Poor Luke – he's been under such horrible stress recently. I just don't know ... there's a chance he - killed himself - isn't there? That would be just horrible. If people found out he had killed himself, the stain would take years to wear off." She clutched at her pearls.

"Was your husband suicidal, Mrs. Williams?" She crossed her arms and looked down, quite aware of the psychological advantage she had from standing over the woman, playing it for all it was worth.

"He had been depressed. He ... he had been losing money in the market. I don't know if he took money from anyone. But you must understand that even the hint of such a thing would taint our name. You must understand how important our reputation is."

"Is that why you didn't mention his depression to us when we first spoke? At that time you seemed convinced he couldn't possibly have committed suicide."

"I don't know what happened, Detective."

Porter understood that she was treading on slippery ground, that if she wanted to continue the conversation along the course it was taking, she needed Joe present. Silently cursing herself for not bringing him, she uncrossed her arms. "I see. We are investigating all aspects of this case, and I'm sure we'll find the truth soon." She meant it as a warning.

"I'd do just about anything to protect my family, Detective. Do you have a family?"

"No, I don't." She forced herself not to ask the obvious question, the question that would require her to advise Mrs. Williams of her rights. There wasn't enough physical proof to justify that. "I need to speak to Michelle."

Virginia started to protest, then let it die. She raised her voice and called her daughter into the room. Michelle came, slowly, her eyes downcast. "Yes, Mother?"

"Detective Sienna needs to talk to you. Please answer her as truthfully as you can." Virginia rose and swept out, leaving the impression that she couldn't bear to hear what was going to be discussed. Porter turned her attention to Michelle Williams.

The girl was of average height and build, dark haired. Her clothes were of an expensive cut, but worn somewhat uncomfortably. She tried not to look at Porter's face, her eyes darting everywhere but at her. She did not excite Porter's emotions, but it was apparent that she was suppressing herself within a different cover. Porter wondered what Elaine had seen in her.

"Miss Williams. Please, sit down and make yourself comfortable. This will only take a few minutes." Michelle sat, crossing her legs, then uncrossing them. "Tell me about Elaine Jessup."

The reaction was startling. Michelle's head jerked upward, her eyes widening. She stared at Porter open-mouthed for a moment, then blushed a deep red. "Elaine?" Her voice was high-pitched, didn't sound normal.

"Yes. I understand you were involved with her at one time." Porter tried to convince herself that she was asking in order to establish just how domineering Virginia Williams was, but in the back of her mind lurked the knowledge that she also wanted to know about Elaine.

"I – I was younger then, foolish." Her eyes darted toward the kitchen. "It was a mistake to let her talk me into it."

"So you don't consider yourself a lesbian?" Another blush, and a slight hesitation. The eyes went to the door again.

"No. Mother sent me to a wonderful therapist who helped me see how I was being manipulated." The words sounded forced, rehearsed. Porter noted that she had just said mother, not mother and father.

"Do you think Elaine Jessup is capable of blackmail?"

"I guess anyone is capable of anything, given reason enough." Michelle looked at Porter as she spoke, her eyes trying to convey something, but Porter couldn't determine what.

"Thank you for your time, Miss Williams." Porter gave her a card. "If you think of anything that might be helpful, let me know."

Walking away from the house, Porter felt herself shaking with anger at Virginia Williams. It was clear to her that Michelle Williams had been forced to hide behind a veil of acceptance of her mother's wishes. She hoped fervently that Michelle would call her, would be able to talk to her away from her mother's influence.

*   *   *   *   *

"Where the hell you been, Porter?" Joe stood up as she came to her desk. "The lieutenant's ready to spit nails."

"I was talking to the widow Williams again. I've got a sneaking suspicion about her. Nothing I can prove, not yet."

"Well, we're due at the PM in half an hour. You'd better go in an appease Day's feathers before we take off again." Porter sighed and looked up at the closed door of her lieutenant.

"Shit. I hate office politics." Joe shrugged. Porter went and rapped on the door, entering went instructed. Lieutenant Day looked up from his desk and frowned.

"You're late."

"I interviewed Mrs. Williams this morning." Day's frown deepened.

"Why?"

"Because she's a suspect. Because I have reason to believe she should be our prime suspect."

Day looked at her sharply. "What makes you say that?"

"My information to this point indicates that she should be." Porter shrugged. "It would be premature to make further speculation."

"Well, I hope you aren't ignoring other possibles while you follow this line of thought."

"No, sir, I'm not." Porter shifted and slipped her hands into her pockets. "I'm due at the PM, sir."

"Get out of here. And keep me posted. I want this solved, damn it! And if you plan on arresting Mrs. Williams you'd better make damn sure you can make it stick."

"Oh, I will be." On a sudden thought, she asked, "Did you by chance talk to her right after the lab report came out?"

"No. Why do you ask?"

"She said someone here told her over the phone that her husband had been murdered."

"Well, find out who it was and chew his ass. No one should be handing out information like that over the phone."

"Yes, sir." Porter backed out of the office and closed

the door before letting her breath out. Joe was watching for her, grinning and shaking his head. She lifted her middle finger at him, then motioned for him to join her. "Day's an ass," she grumbled as they rode down to the basement in the elevator.

"Yes, but he's an ass with bars." Joe grinned at her. "Maybe he has the hots for you."

"Oh, please." They stepped out into the cool air of the basement level and turned toward the morgue. "I'd as soon chew broken glass."

The coroner greeted them with the wave of a latex gloved hand as they entered the observation area. Luke William's body was already laid out on the table, hugely naked. Porter noted with some disgust that he was extremely hairy. And extremely well endowed, though she'd been told that death had a way of exaggerating a man's size somewhat.

"I understand we're looking for evidence of poisoning by tubocurarine chloride," Dr. James Grey said cheerfully. "That shouldn't be too difficult, spectrographically speaking. I don't expect to find too much physical evidence, but then curare mimics heart failure."

Porter nodded and reached for a mask. Joe already had his on. She smiled to herself. He was even more susceptible to the smell than she was. She almost enjoyed the visual aspects of an autopsy, which she supposed made her twisted in some way or another. It fascinated her to see the variety of colors and textures of the parts of the human body.

Grey put on his own mask and face shield, then turned on the microphone over the autopsy table and began to speak. "Case number 125-28-3546, Luke Williams. The body is that of a well-nourished fifty-six year old Caucasian male with gray hair and blue eyes. The body is 71 inches long and weighs two hundred fifty nine pounds."

Porter watched with fascination as Grey examined the body, noting the needle marks on both thighs. After his external examination was complete, he picked up a scalpel and made a Y incision in the torso. Porter glanced at Joe as he made a sound at the first slice of the scalpel, a sound almost like pain.

"He's dead, Joe. He doesn't feel a thing."

"Yeah, well I do. No matter how many times I watch this, it still hurts to think about."

Dr. Grey put aside his scalpel and spread open the incision, then picked up an electric saw. The smell of burning bone as he cut through the ribcage assailed Porter's nose and made her wince. It reminded her of trips to the dentist, of drills and cavities and things she didn't like to think about.

A little later, James looked up from his examination of the heart and commented, "Advanced vascular sclerosis. This guy should have been in for by-pass surgery a long time ago."

"Could it have been a heart attack?" Joe was staring at the heart laying on the metal table, neatly sliced into segments. James shook his head.

"No. Definitely not a heart attack." He bent back to his work. A while later, he made a noise.

"What?"

"Looks like your man died of respiratory failure. That's consistent with curare poisoning. The diaphragm is paralyzed within seconds of an IM or IV injection. I'll have to get an analysis from the lab on the liver, that and the spectrographic analysis ought to clinch it."

"How long did it take him to die?" Porter cocked her head, amazed that something that looked like a pile of fat to her could yield such exact results.

"Not long. A matter of minutes perhaps." The rest of the autopsy was efficient and routine, and when it was over, Porter and Joe both left the room and headed for the showers. It was an automatic reaction; Porter scrubbed herself zealously under water as hot as she could stand it, then dried off and got dressed again.

She could still smell the body, but she didn't subscribe to the practice many detectives used of snorting pepper or rubbing Vicks under their noses to rid themselves of the smell. She let it stay, to remind her that she was investigating the death of a human being, someone who had once been upright and walking around just as she was.

There was a message on her desk when she returned saying that Margaret Carey had called.

Smiling to herself, Porter dialed the number on the pink slip.

"Pharmacy, Dr. Carey speaking."

"This is Detective Sienna. I got your message." There was a chuckle on the other end of the phone.

"Really. Well, I happened to be logging some records on the computer this morning and I didn't see any missing tubocurarine chloride." Porter slumped. Of course it wouldn't be that easy. "Sorry I couldn't be of more help."

"Well, thank you for looking."

"You could repay me with lunch one day." Her tone was casual. Porter smiled despite herself.

"All right. I can probably manage that." She said goodbye and hung up, then crossed her arms and watched Joe making his way over. "No luck on missing drugs at the hospital," she told him.

"Did you think we'd be so lucky?" He responded with a wry grin. "What next?"

"I think I ought to go check John Archibald's account, see how much Williams stole from him. He's our second best suspect at his point."

"Okay. I'll see what I can dig up on life insurance, debts, that sort of thing." Porter nodded. Joe was good at the drudge work. He acted like he enjoyed it. She thought he had visions of becoming a private investigator.

"Fine with me."

She paused outside the building to smoke a

cigarette, thinking of the best way to approach Elaine. She could either try to apologize, or she could be official and pretend nothing had ever happened between them.

That was something she doubted she could pull off. So apologizing was the only option. Porter hated apologizing, especially when she knew she had been stupid. She finished her smoke and walked quickly to her car.

Chapter IX.

The receptionist recognized her when she approached the desk and stood up. "Ms. Jessup is in a meeting."

"Is that a real meeting or an I don't want to talk to that detective again meeting?" Porter tried to smile disarmingly.

"It's real enough," the receptionist replied. "If you'll have a seat, she should be through shortly."

Porter sat and drank the coffee she was offered and tried to act nonchalant. Twenty minutes later, a door came open and a group of people filed out. Elaine glanced her way and saw her, and turned pale. Porter stood and started toward her, forcing herself to remain impassive. Without a word, Elaine went to her office. Porter followed, closing the door behind her. Elaine sat down and shuffled some papers.

"What can I do for you, detective?" Her voice was strained, sounding angry behind the veneer of politeness.

"Elaine - I'm sorry. About last night."

Elaine looked up at her. "You had no right...."

"I know I had no right. I don't know what got into me." Porter sighed. "Yes, I do. My ex-lover was a horrible cheat. I was reacting to her, not to you. I don't care who you sleep with."

"You could have fooled me." Elaine wasn't going to let her off so easily. "You made me look like an idiot in front of Toby, trying to defend myself."

"I'm sorry. I really am. I've just - I had a bad day yesterday."

"Having a bad day is not an excuse for the things you said."

Porter looked at the ceiling. "Virginia Williams accused you of threatening her."

"What? That's ridiculous. That woman doesn't know when to quit. It's been three god damned years and she still won't let it go."

"Why didn't you tell me about Michelle Williams? You should have known it might have bearing on the case." Elaine stood and crossed to stare out the window.

"I don't like to think about Michelle. It hurts too much." She was silent for a while, then turned suddenly and leaned against the windowsill. "Michelle was twenty-three. I was thirty-eight. I suppose I should have known better, but I didn't. I loved her more than any woman I had ever been with. And she loved me. I believe that to this day."

"Then what happened?"

"Virginia Williams happened. She found out somehow, I don't know how. I was still trying to be discreet in those days. She got hold of Michelle, dragged her to about a dozen different psychiatrists trying to 'cure' her. Hell, brainwash her is more like it. And it worked. Michelle told me she never wanted to see me again and moved to Raleigh."

"Were you her first?"

Elaine laughed. "Hardly. I know better than to get involved in initiations. Anyway, Virginia tried to get Luke to fire me and he wouldn't. But Virginia has hated me ever since."

"So she had a good reason to want to frame you?"

Elaine sobered suddenly. "Isn't that a rather strong term? What did she say to you?"

"She accused you of blackmail. She tried to intimate that you were blackmailing Luke Williams."

"How did you know she was lying?" Elaine looked at Porter curiously. Porter blushed as the image of Elaine's blonde curls moving between her legs sprang without summoning to the forefront of her mind.

"She said you came to her house the night you were at my apartment. I knew quite well how you spent that evening, and it wasn't threatening her."

"I see." Elaine had the decency to blush herself. "That was a pleasant evening."

"I am sorry. I just didn't expect you to have another date the night after - I don't know why I didn't, but I didn't."

"It wasn't a date. Toby's just a friend. A straight friend."

"Oh." Porter felt even more ridiculous for her behavior.

"Anyway, I accept your apology." Porter sighed in relief.

"Good. Would it be possible to look at John Archibald's account? I want to see how much is missing from it."

"Sure." She reached over and pulled a file out of the basket on her desk. "Let's see ...." She got out a calculator and started adding figures. "About fifty thousand. Hardly any. To be honest, Porter, it looks like Luke had started replacing some of what he had taken. I've been going over these accounts again, and there are positive errors in just the last week or so."

"Like he'd had enough and wanted to repay what he'd taken?"

"Exactly."

Porter reflected on this for a moment. "Do you think Virginia Williams knew about the embezzlement?"

"I wouldn't be surprised if she didn't put him up to it."

"Really."

"Luke was driven; driven to maintain a lifestyle he couldn't afford for a woman he didn't love. He was reckless in the market because that's the only thing he had any control over. Virginia was in charge of everything else." Elaine tapped her pen against her blotter. "He might have finally killed himself just to get away from her."

"I suppose that's possible." Porter glanced away. "Look, I know I don't deserve this, but would you go out to dinner with me tonight?"

"You mean actually go out in public?" Porter nodded. "I don't see why not. I've had a cancellation...." When Porter reddened, she laughed. "I'm only kidding. I won't pretend that I don't date more than one woman at a time. But I'm hardly booked solid."

"I've never - it's always been one at a time for me," Porter responded slowly. "I guess I never could get the hang of dating. I tended to find someone I was attracted to and keep them around from the first date on."

"Well, I hope you don't look at me that way, because I'm not ready to get caught again. Michelle was terribly damaging to my psyche."

"As Beth was to mine. Maybe I've learned my lesson. I'm not going to reserve a U-Haul anytime soon, regardless." Both women laughed at the joke. "Why don't I pick you up at, say, seven?"

"All right." Elaine scribbled something down on her notepad and tore the sheet off. It was a Hanes Park address, near the club. "I'll be ready at seven."

"You live here?" Porter swallowed, starting to feel out of her league. A Jaguar and a Land Rover, and now an address that was in the richest part of town.

"I inherited it." Elaine raised an eyebrow. "Is there a problem?"

"No. I'm just thinking that maybe I was a bit foolish in my career choice."

"You're very good at what you do."

"Are you referring to my job?" Porter raised her eyes and caught the laughter in Elaine's.

"This time, yes I am. I'll see you tonight."

"Tonight." Porter left the office and sat in her car staring across the empty field next door for a long while. She couldn't stay away from Elaine Jessup, no matter how hard she tried. She just hoped that, unlike the moth, she would be able to keep herself from expiring against the brilliance of Elaine's flame.

*   *   *   *   *

"Sienna!" Porter glanced up as someone called her from the front of the office. "Someone here to see you." Throwing Joe a confused shrug, she went out to the reception area. Michelle Williams sat nervously on the institutional couch above which hung the FBI ten most wanted list photographs.

"Miss Williams," Porter exclaimed, pleasantly surprised. Michelle stood up, tension obvious on her face.

"Could we - go somewhere - and talk?"

"Sure, let me get my cigarettes and we'll go

outside." She dashed back to her desk and picked up her Marlboro's, and winked at Joe. "Our luck may be changing."

She accompanied Michelle to the front of the station, then lit a cigarette and waited for her to start talking. After fidgeting for a few moments, she sighed. "I couldn't talk to you before, not with my mother in the other room."

"I gathered there was a problem," Porter responded.

"I - you really threw me, asking about Elaine."

"Well, she has made accusations against your father, embezzlement charges, and your mother has made counter charges. I wanted to – get as much background on the animosity between them as I could."

Michelle hung her head. "Mother despises Elaine. She blames her for my being a lesbian."

"So you still are?"

"Of course I am. It isn't something you can cure, despite what I was told repeatedly during my counseling. I just wasn't strong enough to stand up to mother, and father wasn't going to back me up. So I played her game and left. Elaine hates me, I'm sure she does. But I had to do what I did." Porter understood, too well, what she meant. She had allowed her relationship with Beth to weaken until it was beyond salvation because of a fear of being found out at work.

"Your mother seems a little – overbearing at times."
Michelle laughed critically. "A little? If she can't
control you, she destroys you."

"So there's no love lost between the two of you."

"No, none. It wouldn't surprise me if she killed
Daddy."

Porter looked at her sharply. "Do you know
something I should?"

"I doubt it. Although ... I think she was having an
affair."

"With whom?"

"I don't know. I called last week, and it was
obvious I had interrupted something, I could hear her
telling someone to keep quiet. Daddy was out of town
at the time." This was interesting information. "She's
so concerned about the family reputation. I personally
don't give a shit for our reputation. We're so
dysfunctional it's amazing we even qualify as a
family." Her tone was bitter.

"Would you be willing to make a statement –"

"No! No, I can't cross her. I have a lover, I have my
own life to think about. I'm just now finding some
sort of peace. I can't risk bringing her down on my
head again." Michelle Williams was shaking. Porter
finished her cigarette and nodded.

"I understand. Thank you for coming to me with
this."

"Do you ... do you know Elaine?" Porter felt a flush
steal up her cheeks.

"I've met her during the investigation, yes."

"Does she seem – has she gotten over me yet?" Michelle was giving her an odd look.

"I don't know," Porter lied. "We haven't discussed her personal life in detail."

Another odd look. "Well, she's a wonderful woman. She deserves to be with someone who'll treat her right. Better than I did."

Why tell me? Porter wondered, then shook her head. Gaydar could penetrate even the best disguise. "I'll remember that." She watched as Michelle Williams walked away, then turned and went back inside.

"Well?" Joe asked her as she sat down. "What was that all about?"

"Michelle Williams," Porter replied. "She thinks her mother was having an affair. She practically accused her of killing her father."

"Something else to look into," Joe grumped good-naturedly. "Just when we thought things were going to get easy."

"Oh, please."

"Nothing interesting on my end. I'm ready to go home."

"Yeah, me too." Porter tidied up her desk and paused to look over at her partner. "I think tomorrow we might want to put the screws to Virginia Williams."

"Do you have a motive? What pretty story are you

planning on weaving for her?" Joe leaned forward.

"I'm not sure yet. But I feel it in my gut; she's guilty."

"Humph. We'll see." He stood and gave her a mock salute. "Good night, Sherlock."

Chapter X.

Porter pulled into the driveway of a large rectangular two-story brick house at five minutes to seven. She put the car in park and stared at the building; it was modest by Hanes Park standards which meant it was only worth three or four hundred thousand dollars.

The porch light was on even though it wouldn't be dark for almost three more hours. Porter counted to ten before getting out of the car. She noted that there was an identical sign by the walkway as at the Williams' house. However, this one was for a different company. Porter couldn't help but wonder if Jamie Black Landscaping was a woman-owned business. It seemed Elaine's style.

Realizing that she was putting off going to the door, Porter reassured herself that she wasn't in over her head and walked up to the porch. White wicker furniture sat in a grouping to the left, the right portion of the porch filled with plants. The front door stood open. Understanding the mute invitation to come on in, Porter forced herself to ring the doorbell anyway. Elaine's voice echoed from the recesses of the building, telling her to come inside.

Standing in the foyer, Porter marveled at how similar the decorating was to her father's house. The difference was that Elaine was slowly adding her own touch to the interior. Here and there were obvious examples of a newer decorator; a print where once a painting would have hung, a chair upholstered in what looked like cowhide complete with spots sitting next to an antique hall table.

A curving staircase led from the right side of the foyer to the second story. To the left and kitty-corner to the front door was another door which appeared to lead to a hallway. Porter heard movement from that door and a moment later Elaine appeared, fixing an earring as she moved toward her guest. She wore a pale pink silk pantsuit with a white light cotton jacket over it. Her hair was pulled back along the sides with cloisonné combs.

"Come on in, don't stand in the door all night."

"I was admiring the decor." Porter took a moment to admire her hostess, thinking how wonderfully soft Elaine looked.

"In the foyer? Bull. Come into the living room and have a drink." She indicated double French doors to the left then went and pulled them open and stepped through. Porter followed mutely.

The living room ran the width of the house, perhaps fifty feet by twenty. A baby grand piano dominated a large bay window at the front of the room, directly across from where they had come in. The carpeting was white, the walls a light pearl gray. The furniture was placed the same as every other living room Porter had ever seen in Hanes Park, a sofa with two round end tables in front of a large fireplace, a wing chair in a paisley print and an arm chair with leather upholstery and gleaming brass tacking on one side and a loveseat in a pattern matching the sofa to the other. A low butler's table served as a coffee table.

At the far end of the room was a bridge table and four chairs, flanked by two tall bookcases. A portable bar stood against the wall nearest the fireplace, lined with cut crystal decanters and glasses.

Elaine moved to the bar and poured two drinks, then offered one to Porter, who accepted and took a sip to mask her discomfort. Classical music filled the room from speakers hidden behind large potted plants. The portrait over the fireplace was an oil of Elaine and her parents and a remarkably ugly dog.

"Would you prefer the den? It's a little less intimidating." Elaine was studying her as she nodded. "All right." They walked back into the entry, then through double doors at the opposite end of the foyer into a room lined with built in bookshelves. A desk against the front window was overflowing with papers.

Going to yet another door, Elaine motioned Porter through into the den. It was a cozier room, paneled entirely in oak, with a black leather living room suite arranged in front of a home entertainment center. Elaine walked over to it and pressed a button, and the music filled this room.

"I like this room," Porter said, feeling overwhelmed.

"This is the only one I've redecorated. It used to look like a refuge for pipe smoking old men, which it was." Elaine sank down onto the sofa and Porter sat in the chair. "I'm glad you like it."

"You have this whole place to yourself?"

"Yes. I don't mind. It's easier to keep clean with just me." There was a pause. "So, where are we going for dinner?"

"Britain's." It was as chic as Porter could afford, and the only place she'd been able to get reservations. "Our table is for eight."

"Then we have time to relax. I should show you the rest of the house."

"That's all right. I'll see it eventually." Elaine sank back and studied her over the rim of her glass.

"It bothers you that I'm well off?" It wasn't really a question. Porter shrugged.

"It bothers me more that you're Society."

"Not all of us choose to drop out just because we don't fit the stereotype. And I'm not trying to say you're any the less for doing so. I'm just saying I still feel comfortable here."

- 118 -

Porter's anger died as quickly as it had arisen. "My road wasn't as clear-cut as yours seems to have been."

"We all have our crosses to bear." Elaine fell silent for a while. "How is your investigation going?"

"We anticipate making an arrest soon." Porter hated falling back on the trite police phrases she so often used with the press, but she didn't know quite what else to say to Elaine.

"Then you have a suspect?"

"We are looking at a particular suspect, yes. I'd really rather not talk about it."

"Then what would you like to talk about?"

"How long have you known you were a lesbian?" Elaine's lips curled into a smile and she brushed her hand across the forehead.

"Ah, my coming out story. Would you believe I was married for ten years?" When Porter looked startled, she laughed. "Well, I was. I got married at eighteen, just as a rebellion. I was the original rebel without a clue. Had a baby at twenty and another at twenty-one."

"Where are your children now?" It seemed so unlikely that Elaine would have children.

"Joshua just graduated from Carolina and is working in Cary. Jennifer will graduate next year. She's majoring in finance. I think she wants to follow in my footsteps. She lives with a nice girl named Stephanie, to the eternal chagrin of her father. I like to tease him about it, seeing as how he raised them from the time they were seven and eight."

"So you lost custody when you divorced?"

"I didn't ask for custody. I knew I wasn't cut out to be a mother. It was better for them to live with their father and stepmother. I went through a difficult time after my divorce." Elaine paused to take a drink. "I'm not very proud of it, but I had my first lesbian affair while I was still married. In fact, it was less than a year after Stephanie was born. I was so shocked that it took me almost seven years to try it again. Then I knew I had to leave Eric and make it on my own."

"I've always known, I think. At least from the time I was old enough to put a word to how I felt." Porter pursed her lips. "I can't imagine being with a man."

"It's hard for me to imagine sometimes. If it wasn't for the children, I'd suspect my marriage was some ten year delusion on my part." Elaine consulted her watch. "We should get going if we want to get there on time."

*   *   *   *   *

Over appetizers, Elaine started talking again. "It must be difficult to hide your sexuality, being a police officer," she commented. Porter glanced at her.

"Yes, it is. Beth couldn't stand it that I insisted on acting so straight. You might have noticed that I have a two bedroom apartment. She had her own bedroom. I suppose I got more paranoid after I made detective - wearing plain clothes made it harder to hide."

"So you make a stab at passing. I noticed you didn't seem very comfortable in your work clothes. You dress more, I don't know, sensually when you're off duty."

Porter took a sip of her wine, then watched the liquid moving as she twirled the glass stem between her fingertips. "How did you know?"

"It was so obvious to me. I don't know exactly how. Call it gaydar if you want. I'm sure you get that once in a while."

"More so since Beth left. I don't think I was so sensitive to other lesbians before that."

Elaine smiled and touched her finger to her lips. "Shh. You don't want anyone to hear you say the 'L' word, do you?"

"I suppose I deserve that. You know, I thought when I left the club set I'd be free to be myself. You seem much freer than I am." Porter frowned at the truth in her own words.

"Well, it took a long time for me to get to this point. I was in the closet while the children were younger, while my father was still alive. You know how important family reputations are." Porter made a noise. "Well, they are."

"Virginia Williams kept going on about her family reputation. It's sad, isn't it? People are more concerned with their good name than with catching a

- 121 -

killer."

Elaine nodded and sipped at her wine. Porter looked across the table at her, and realized with a sudden shock that she was beautiful. Really beautiful, not the made up beauty that so many aging debutantes possess, but an inner beauty that showed through in her face.

She remembered the way Elaine had taken control of her body and felt a tremor of desire pass through her. She sought to regain her composure by twirling her wine glass again, but it was too late. A growing wetness between her thighs reminded her that she was, in fact, highly attracted to the woman opposite her.

"You got quiet all of a sudden." Elaine was studying her with a bemused expression. Porter felt a foot touch her calf under the table. "Is something the matter?"

"No." Her throat was dry. "I'm sure a lot of women are speechless around you."

"Oh, a few. Now and then. I've usually done more than sit at a table with them, though." She made a noise almost like a giggle. "You're blushing again."

"You are one of the few people in the world who can make me do that," Porter grumbled, ducking her head. A moment later, she looked up to see Elaine's eyes fixed on her with hungry intent. "If you don't stop looking at me that way in public I'm going to have to arrest you. You're dangerous."

"Hmmm. If you arrest me, will I get to see you use your handcuffs?" She raised an eyebrow questioningly and tilted her head as her mouth quirked into a lascivious smile.

"I ought to. That grin should be registered as a deadly weapon."

Elaine laughed. "Poor woman. Do you think you'll survive dinner, or should I take you into the ladies' room before our entrees arrive?"

Porter resisted the temptation to throw a bacon-wrapped scallop at her, settling for a warning growl. Elaine seemed to be enjoying her role as temptress, and settled back in her chair with an innocent look on her face while her foot, devoid of its shoe, climbed Porter's leg.

Niagara Falls isn't this wet, Porter groaned to herself as another rush of warmth struck her groin. Apparently satisfied with her handiwork, Elaine straightened up and resumed eating. Porter squirmed uncomfortably in her seat for the rest of the meal, trying to make polite conversation when all she really wanted to do was tell the woman opposite her exactly what she wanted to do when they got back to her house.

After dinner and an excruciating drive during which Elaine's fingers kept sneaking their way onto her thigh, Porter turned into the driveway of Elaine's house and parked the car.

"Come in and have a nightcap," Elaine said

innocently. Porter was too far gone to even consider refusing, and she had a sneaking suspicion Elaine knew this. It amazed her that she could so willingly fall under someone's spell, could allow herself to be led the way Elaine was leading her.

Accepting a bourbon and water, she sat in the den and watched the sway of Elaine's hips as they crossed the room to turn the stereo on. She realized then that she was sweating. Elaine returned to sit beside her, draping her arm casually across the back of the sofa behind Porter's shoulders.

"So, what should we talk about now?" Elaine's voice danced around the edges as it had the first time she had spoken to Porter. Porter found it increasingly difficult to concentrate on anything other than the tiny gold cross hanging in the cleavage of Elaine's blouse.

"What do you think Carolina's chances at a bowl bid are this year?"

Elaine laughed. "If that's all you can come up with, you must be worse off than I thought. Poor baby."

"I seem to be in a bad way where you're concerned," Porter admitted slowly. "I can't figure it out."

"It's simple. You see something you like. What's so hard to understand about that?"

"You aren't – my type at all. I mean, physically you are, but the rest...." Porter swallowed from her drink to cover her lack of words. "I'm not accustomed to bottoming for my lovers."

"Oh, is that it? Well, I can be pretty demanding. I like being in control of the pace." She moved her hand into Porter's hair, running her fingers through it with graceful motions. Porter sat her glass down and leaned back, relishing the touch. "You need a woman to pamper you. Someone to relieve you of the pressure of performing. I can do that for you."

Her fingers moved to Porter's neck, stroking with long, soft strokes until Porter's head fell back and she shut her eyes, her entire being floating beneath that gentle pressure.

She heard the rustling of silk as Elaine bent to kiss her. It was a quiet kiss, the sort one long time lover gives her partner, and it caused an explosion in Porter's stomach unlike anything she had ever known. Turning her head to prolong the contact of their lips, she opened her eyes to two glowing blue gems that caught her and pulled her in.

Without a word, Elaine stood and held out her hand. Porter took it and allowed herself to be led through the study, up the curving staircase, and down a wide hall to yet another set of double doors. Elaine pushed them open and pulled Porter inside her room.

Porter hardly saw the room itself. What struck her with a force not unlike lightning was the feeling of comfort it exuded. This was a room in which someone lived and loved, unlike the sterile coldness of Porter's own room. She had an impression of white and green, but instead of being icy, it enveloped her and made her feel secure.

Elaine was standing before her, her hands in her hair, pulling her in for another kiss. They stood together for the space of a dozen pounding heartbeats, or perhaps a dozen dozen, then she lifted her head and dropped her hands to Porter's shoulders. Her thumbs traced Porter's collarbones.

Porter stood still, unwilling to break the touch, unable to take command. She understood instinctively that this was a dance, that Elaine would lead and she follow. Perhaps later the tempo would change and so would their places, but for now she was content to give herself into Elaine's care.

Slowly, Elaine unbuttoned Porter's blouse and pulled it from her shoulders, dropping it to the floor. She unfastened the bra and slid it down Porter's arms, freeing her breasts. Porter's nipples were already hard, had been for some time. With the palms of her hands, Elaine moved slowly back up Porter's arms to her shoulders, hesitated, then moved down across her chest, circling inward over her breasts.

Porter caught her breath and pressed forward involuntarily as she felt the warmth of Elaine's hands on her nipples. Without breaking the steady rhythm of her movement, Elaine slid her fingers around the curves of Porter's breasts and down her sides to the waist band of her slacks, then to her spine and up along the indentation of her back. At her shoulders, she stepped in and pressed her lips against Porter's waiting mouth once again, this time reaching with her tongue to dip inside, to taste and take what strength Porter had left.

The silk of her blouse was cool against Porter's bare skin, which raged with inner heat. Porter lifted her arms to Elaine's waist and returned the kiss, searching, hungry. Elaine lifted her head away and smiled tenderly, then turned with Porter still in her arms and gently lowered her to the bed.

Her hands were firm as they unfastened Porter's slacks and slid them down her legs and off. Then she leaned over and kissed the hollow of her throat, her tongue drawing a lazy line around each breast before she moved to a nipple, enclosing it in her mouth and nipping at it tenderly. Porter groaned. She turned to the other breast and repeated the process, then continued to moved down until she knelt at last between Porter's legs, her breath hot through the fabric of Porter's briefs.

She kissed all along the insides of Porter's thighs, pausing now and then to let her breath caress the moistness still hidden by cotton fabric. Porter wanted to reach down and grab her hair, wanted to pull her mouth hard against her, but she couldn't move. Finally, Elaine slipped the panties off and let her tongue burrow into the wet tangle of pubic hair.

Porter's groan was louder and more heartfelt. Satisfied with her state of arousal, Elaine parted hair and lips with her hands and buried her face firmly against Porter's center. Her tongue danced in the wetness, circling and teasing at her clitoris, touching, just barely entering her.

"Stop teasing," Porter pleaded. She felt Elaine smile, then there was a melting pleasure as her lips fastened securely against her clitoris, sucking and licking until she could no longer control herself. With a strangled scream she came, her back arching off the bed, her hands clawing into the coverlet in spastic motions. Elaine moved with her, taking what she gave until she collapsed, spent.

Elaine wiped her face against Porter's thigh and rested her chin at the top of her curly triangle. "Feeling a little better?"

"Ungh," was the only sound Porter could manage. Elaine stood, and it was only then that Porter realized she was still fully clothed. She tried to struggle to a sitting position, but Elaine stopped her.

"Just relax." She began to undress herself. When she was at last naked, she pulled back the covers and motioned for Porter to join her beneath them. Once they were snuggled together, Porter nestled comfortably in Elaine's arms, Elaine kissed her lips with quiet determination. "Recovered yet?"

"Yes." Sensing that the tempo had changed, Porter took the lead. It was to be her dance now, and she was eager to begin it. Turning so that they lay front to front, Porter used her weight to press Elaine onto her back. She kissed her lips, her forehead, her chin, then moved down to suckle at her erect nipples.

Elaine moaned softly and ran her hands through Porter's hair, feeding each nipple to her with a quiet "yes". Porter positioned herself between Elaine's thighs so that they now lay groin to groin, and began to move against her. She dropped her head to continue her hungry attack on Elaine's breasts, sucking them until it was Elaine who was pleading with her to stop teasing.

Sliding a hand between their bodies, Porter delved carefully into Elaine's wetness, letting it cover her fingers as she explored the lines and folds that Elaine pressed up against her. "Please," Elaine whispered finally. "Please, don't make me wait any longer."

Smiling, Porter filled her with two fingers and began a steady in and out motion that brought sudden movement from Elaine's hips. She raised up to a kneeling position and applied herself more vigorously. Elaine was groaning, her head turning side to side, her eyes closed. Porter thrust against her, feeling her tighten against her fingers with each thrust as if to keep her inside.

Elaine's hands groped for some purchase, and when she failed to make contact with Porter, she gripped the headboard, lifting her hips against Porter's hand. Porter felt the orgasm gathering within her and bent once more to her breast. With a long scream of pleasure Elaine bucked up from the bed, wrapped her legs around Porter's waist, and exploded into climax.

Afterwards, she lay gasping for air as Porter moved carefully back into her arms. They rested in silence for a few minutes, then Elaine turned to Porter and began to move her hands once more over her body. Porter sighed. She liked the way this dance was going.

Chapter XI.

"You certainly are chipper this morning," Joe commented as Porter sat her coffee cup down and flipped a page on the autopsy report.

"I had a good evening." Porter smiled to herself at the memory of waking up nestled against Elaine's back, feeling the rise of fall of her breathing. She returned to the report before her. The lab results indicated the presence of curare in Luke Williams' body. So it was for certain that he did inject himself with the drug, and died as a result.

Setting the file aside for the moment, Porter pulled out her notes. She looked through them, trying to make some more sense of them than she had been able to before, looking for something she had missed. She found herself looking at the notes from the second interview with Virginia Williams.

Something bothered her, something Mrs. Williams had said. Curious, Porter picked up the phone and called the switchboard. A few questions confirmed what she had suspected; no one had spoken to

Virginia Williams on the morning following her husband's death.

"Joe?" He made a noise. "Do you remember the second time we interviewed Mrs. Williams? She knew her husband had been murdered and that he had been poisoned."

"She said some numbskull here told her that."

Porter grinned. "But we had just gotten the lab report ourselves. The only people who could have told her were the two of us and Lieutenant Day. And he says he didn't talk to her, and I just confirmed with the switchboard that no one else did either."

"Circumstantial. She could have guessed." Joe was good at playing the devil's advocate. "But it's a good start."

"She said yesterday she'd do almost anything to protect her family. Do you think she'd murder?"

"Where did she get the curare?" Porter's first thought was John Archibald. He had denied being close to Williams, yet had hesitated when asked about Virginia. *Could he have been the person Michelle heard her mother telling to be quiet?*

"If she was having an affair, she may have wanted him out of the way so that she could be with her lover. If he was a doctor...."

Joe raised an eyebrow at her. "How do you know it was a he?"

Porter just glowered at him. "Do you think we should have another chat with John Archibald?"

"Archibald? He doesn't seem her type. But it might be worth a shot." Porter nodded.

"Both of us this time."

*   *   *   *   *

Dr. Archibald didn't seem happy to see the two detectives when he came into his office and sat down. Porter noted that he kept glancing at the wall clock. "What can I do for you now," he asked.

"Dr. Archibald, in our previous conversation you indicated that you weren't particularly close to Mr. Williams." Porter made a show of referring to her notes.

"That's correct." *He's not going to say anything he isn't forced to,* Porter thought. *He's hiding something.*

"How about his wife? Were you close to her?"

"No." He answered quickly, too quickly for Porter. She pressed him, sensing that he was getting nervous.

'I see that she and your wife were classmates in college. Have you known her that long?"

Archibald ran a hand across his forehead and adjusted his glasses. "Yes."

The yes and no answers were very telling. "Were you in love with her?"

"What?" John Archibald started to rise from his chair, then apparently thought better of it and sank back down. "Of course not. I'm married."

He answered that question as if it were asked in the

present tense, not the past. Let's see how he responds to a more direct approach. "Dr. Archibald, were you having an affair with Virginia Williams at the time of her husband's death?"

He went white. "No!"

"Here's my theory," Porter went on, as if he hadn't spoken. "You and Mrs. Williams were engaged in an affair. It was decided that Luke Williams stood in the way of that affair, and the two of you plotted to kill him. You obtained a supply of tubocurarine chloride, which Mrs. Williams used to contaminate Luke Williams' allergy medication."

"Absolutely not!" Archibald was sweating. Joe broke in.

"Dr. Archibald, at this time I think it necessary to advise you of your rights." He listed the Miranda rights, asking after each if the man before him understood. Archibald responded with a stunned 'yes' each time. "If you wish, we can continue this conversation after you have had the opportunity to contact your lawyer."

"Are you arresting me?"

"Not at this time. However, I feel you aren't being completely truthful with us." Porter studied his expression. He looked like he was completely in shock. She began to have an uncomfortable feeling that she had come to the wrong conclusion.

"I swear to God I wasn't involved with Virginia." Porter held up her hand to stop him.

"Are you waiving your rights to have a lawyer present during questioning?"

"Yes! I didn't do anything! I admit, I love Virginia, I have for a long time. But she isn't aware of that. No one is aware of that!" There were tears in his eyes. "I would never help anyone kill anybody. I couldn't...."

Joe and Porter exchanged glances. Joe shifted in his chair and leaned forward. "Are you saying, Dr. Archibald, that you categorically deny any involvement in the death of Luke Williams?"

Archibald stared at him. "Yes. Of course I deny it."

"Thank you, Dr. Archibald." Porter rose. "We'll be in touch."

They left him with his head in his hands. Outside the building, Porter reached for a cigarette and shook her head. "Damn. I thought we had him."

"It was a good thought, Porter. Now what do we do?"

Porter wasn't ready to give up on the idea just yet. "I say we put the same scenario to Virginia Williams."

"And if she denies it as well?"

"Maybe we can get something out of the maid."
They got in Joe's car and headed into Hanes Park.

* * * * *

Michelle Williams let them in. She gave Porter a tiny, knowing smile and led them into the living room. A few minutes later, Virginia Williams made her entrance. She still wore black. Porter was beginning to think her show of mourning was a little too obvious.

"Do you have any news, any at all?" She was playing the bereaved widow to the hilt. "This is beginning to wear on all of us, wondering who could have done such a thing."

"Well, Mrs. Williams, perhaps we can clear that up." Porter kept her voice neutral. "We've just come from speaking with John Archibald."

Virginia Williams' expression didn't change. "John? What about him?"

"We know you were having an affair," Porter said, deliberately trying to suggest that John Archibald was the one with whom she was having it. Virginia went pale, but only a little bit.

"I don't know what you're talking about."

"Come now, Mrs. Williams. You haven't given us a straight answer to anything we've asked yet. Don't you think its time you did?" Joe matched Porter's neutrality, but his gruff male voice managed to sound a little threatening anyway.

"Surely you aren't suggesting that I had anything to do with Luke's death?" Her shock didn't ring true with Porter. "Why, that's the most preposterous ... outrageous.... How dare you!"

"How did you know your husband had been poisoned before anyone from our department told you that he had?" Virginia was looking between the two of them, her expression one of righteous indignation.

"Get out of my house. I won't sit here and be subjected to such ridiculous insinuations."

"Mrs. Williams...." Porter didn't want to be forced to arrest her, not yet. They needed to know where the curare had come from. "If your affair was not related to your husband's death, then why won't you tell us who the other party is?"

"Anything else you may wish to ask of me, you may ask of James Murray, my attorney," she huffed. "Now get out of here or I'll have you thrown out."

Grim-faced, Porter went to the door. She turned back for a moment, and the look on Virginia Williams' face was something so close to animal hatred that it almost frightened her. Without another word, Porter stepped outside into the warm fresh air.

"What do you think?" Joe trotted alongside her as she strode to the car. "Does she get the Emmy?"

"She gets the Emmy, the Tony, and the Oscar," Porter growled in return. "Not capable of murder my ass."

"Too bad your lead at the hospital didn't pan out." Joe opened his door and started to climb in. Porter stopped dead, her hand on the top of the car. *The hospital. Of course!*

"Joe, head toward Irving Hospital." She jumped into her seat and reached for the seatbelt.

"What's clicking in that brain of yours?" He put the

car into reverse and started down the driveway.

Porter replayed her conversation with Margaret Carey. The crash of a box falling as she said Virginia Williams' name, the haughty look on the face of the pharmacy assistant ... only it hadn't been haughtiness, it had been fear. If she hadn't been so taken with Dr. Carey, she might have realized it sooner. Porter cursed herself mentally. Twice in the investigation she had been too preoccupied with her own thoughts to notice important clues.

"There are two young men working in the pharmacy," she said. "And I think one of them bears our immediate attention."

They pulled into the circular front drive of the hospital and parked. Porter was out of the car almost before it had stopped. Joe caught up with her in the hall. "Slow down, for chrissake!"

"I don't want this kid disappearing."

Margaret Carey looked up with a smile as the pair came around the corner. She leaned on the ledge of her window and put her chin on her fist. "Hey there, detective."

"Dr. Carey. I need to speak to one of your assistants." Porter looked past her and spotted the young man she remembered from her previous visit. "Him."

Drawing her brows together in confusion, Margaret turned to see who Porter was pointing at. "Darren, come over here a minute."

Darren turned, saw Porter and Joe, and went white. He stood still for just a moment, then came barreling for the pharmacy door. Caught off guard, Porter allowed him to get through the door and several steps down the hall before she could react.

She launched herself after him, colliding with him and throwing him against the wall, pinning him in place. "In a hurry to get somewhere?"

"Lemme go," he squealed in terror. "I don't know anything, I swear, I don't know anything!"

Porter shook her head as she reached for her cuffs. Joe came strolling up, looking faintly amused by the whole situation. "Don't know anything about what, son?" His voice was tinged with laughter.

"You have the right to remain silent," Porter intoned, wanting to Mirandize the young man before he started babbling things they might want to use. She finished with her speech and asked if he understood. He simply stared at her. "Do you understand your rights?" She asked again.

"Yes," he stammered.

"Good. Let's go downtown and have a chat. Joe, take this gentleman to the car." Joe took the man's arm and led him off down the hall. Dusting herself off, Porter turned and went back to the counter. As she suspected, Margaret had been watching her closely.

"Thanks for leaving me short," the pharmacist said with a grimace. "Mind telling me what's going on?"

"Can you do a manual count on your medications? I know, you need a written authorization, signed in triplicate by the administrator, God, and Santa Claus."

Margaret laughed. "Just the administrator. But I'll get on it while you're talking to him. I guess I'm looking for missing vials of tubocurarine chloride, right?"

"Yes. Tell me, did you ever see Darren and Virginia Williams together?" Margaret pursed her lips and considered.

"I think they had lunch once in a while. Darren was a friend of her son's." Porter nodded and turned to go in search of the administrator. She had gone about four steps before Margaret called after her. "That lunch has been upgraded to dinner, you know!"

Turning back around, walking backwards, Porter saluted and smiled, then resumed her forward position and strode off down the hall.

* * * * *

The interrogation room was claustrophobic. Porter paced expectantly behind the table, waiting for Darren Elon to be brought up from booking. Joe sat at the table, tipped back in his chair.

"Relax, Porter. We've got the kid cold."

"But will he give us Williams?" Joe shrugged. A few minutes later, a distraught looking Darren Elon was led into the room. He slumped into his chair, looking almost comical in his white hospital uniform and handcuffs, his fingers smeared black with ink. With him was one of the public defenders.

"Mr. Elon," Joe intoned, leaning forward as Porter took her seat. "You are charged with theft of a controlled substance. Why don't you let us in on why you would steal a vial of tubocurarine chloride?"

Darren looked up at his attorney, who shrugged. "I — I...."

"There is a strong possibility that additional charges will be filed," Porter commented, glancing at her paperwork. "Conspiracy to commit theft, conspiracy to commit murder ... in the very least accessory to murder. The medicine you stole was used to kill a man. Why don't you tell us about that?"

"Mr. Elon is under no requirement to incriminate himself," the attorney responded, sounding bored. "These questions aren't very appropriate."

"We know you associated with Virginia Williams," Porter said, shooting the public defender an evil glance. "We have a witness who has seen the two of you together on more than one occasion. Did you ever associate with Mrs. Williams outside of your work environment?"

"Y-yes." Darren's voice was weak. Porter glanced again at her paperwork. The boy was only twenty-two.

"Have you ever been to her house?"

"Yes."

"Mr. Elon." Joe leaned forward. "Were you engaged in an affair with Mrs. Williams?"

"I don't think – " Porter silenced the attorney with a glare.

"He's hardly incriminating himself with that, Ed." Ed subsided. "Were you having an affair with Virginia Williams, Mr. Elon?" Dumbly, Darren nodded. "Here's what I think happened. You were in love with Mrs. Williams, but she was married. So you decided to get rid of her husband. You stole the tubocurarine chloride from the pharmacy, falsifying the paperwork to make it appear that it had been used, and tainted a vial of Mr. Williams' allergy medication during one of your visits to his house. Is that what happened?"

"No!" Darren suddenly came alive. "No, I didn't! I – she told me it was for the dog, she just wanted to put the dog to sleep, didn't want it to suffer at the vet ... she loved that dog...."

"Darren, I don't think...." Darren cut his lawyer off with a violent motion of his head.

"I didn't kill him. I didn't know she was going to kill him."

"Who? Who told you?" Porter leaned forward expectantly.

"Virginia."

"Did Virginia Williams ask you to steal the medication for her?"

"Yes. She said it was for her dog."

- 142 -

"Didn't you think it a little odd that she not just take her dog to the veterinarians office to be put to sleep?" Porter looked at Ed, who was rolling his eyes, knowing he had lost his client.

"She said she wanted him to be somewhere familiar when he went."

"So you stole the medicine for her. Did you give the medication directly to her?"

Darren looked at her, his eyes full of tears. "If I did, am I going to go to jail?"

"Your attorney and the D.A. can fight over a plea bargain, Mr. Elon. All we want to know is if you gave Mrs. Virginia Williams the medication you stole from Irving Hospital."

There was a long pause. "Yes," he whispered finally. "Yes."

* * * * *

Arrest warrant in hand, Porter rang the doorbell at the Williams house. Michelle Williams again answered the door. "Hi." She said. "Mother told us not to let you back in."

"She did." Porter wasn't amused, but Michelle laughed and moved aside.

"Come on in. Is there anything I can help you with, or do you need Mother?" It was then that she noticed the two uniformed officers standing behind Porter and Joe. "What's going on?"

"We have a warrant for your mother's arrest. Where is she?" Porter stepped into the foyer. Michelle stared at the paper in her hand.

"She actually did it?"

"Where is she, Michelle?" Michelle shook herself as if coming from a dream.

"Upstairs. She went into her room after you left and hasn't been back down. Follow me." With the four police officers behind, Michelle led the way upstairs to a closed door. Stopping, Michelle knocked loudly. "Mother! Mother, it's me."

There was an ominous silence. Michelle tried the door, but it was locked. Porter glanced at Joe, then stepped to the door and pounded on it herself. "Mrs. Williams, open the door. Mrs. Williams!"

"Something's wrong," Michelle muttered.

"Joe, break it."

"Wait." Michelle held up her hand. "I have an easier way." She vanished into the room across the hall and returned with a letter opener. As she expertly jimmied the lock, she explained, "My little sister used to lock herself in the bathroom all the time. All it takes to open these things is the right pressure."

There was a pop, then she straightened and opened the door. Porter stepped cautiously inside, her hand on the grip of her .9mm pistol. "Mrs. Williams?" The room was darkened, shadowy. With a growing sense of dread, Porter edged her way toward the bed on the far side of the large bedroom.

She saw the form on the bed after a few steps, and cursed. "Damn it!" In five strides she was staring down at the pale face of Virginia Williams. Beside her was a syringe and a bottle of medicine. "Damn it, damn it, damn it!"

"Mother?" She sensed Michelle enter the room.

"Joe - keep her out of here." She heard the noises as Joe guided Michelle back out into the hall. Gingerly, Porter pressed her fingers to Virginia's neck; there was no pulse. She hadn't expected to find one. The body was cool to the touch, the beginnings of rigor evident in her chin and neck. She'd been dead at least four hours.

Porter glanced at her watch. It had been five hours since they had last talked to the dead woman. She must have come directly upstairs and killed herself. Looking around, Porter saw an envelope on the bedside table, addressed to her. With trembling hands, she withdrew the single page and read it.

It is unfortunate that it must come to this. If only Luke had been reasonable, all of this could have been avoided and our reputation would not have been imperiled. As it is, this is preferable to a trial. This way there will always be a doubt. You could have prevented this, detective, if you had simply followed your upbringing. You of all people should understand what my reputation means to me.

If you are looking for an admission of guilt, there will be none. I have simply done what I had to do in order to protect my family.

Virginia Williams

Porter folded the note and replaced it in its envelope, then looked down once more at the body of Virginia Williams. Sighing, she turned and walked back to the door, pulling it closed behind her. "Joe," she said wearily, "Call the coroner."

Two hours later, Porter stood in the living room of the Williams house staring angrily out the front window as the stretcher bearing the earthly remains of Mrs. Williams was carried to the waiting van. *I should have known*, she told herself, *I should have guessed she'd do this.* She felt a burning rage, convinced that she should have somehow been able to prevent the suicide.

As she watched the stretcher being loaded into the van, a black jeep pulled into the driveway and parked recklessly on the immaculate lawn. An athletic looking blonde of about thirty leapt from the vehicle and came dashing up to the front door.

Porter turned and walked to meet her, certain that she knew who this was. The woman seemed startled when she saw Porter standing in the open doorway. "Where's Michelle?"

"She's in the kitchen."

Raising her voice, the woman called, "Michelle!" Michelle came running into the hallway, and threw herself into the woman's arms.

"Darling, you're here." Michelle murmured, her face seeking the woman's neck. Porter withdrew as the two kissed, and returned to her position in the living room. A few minutes later, Michelle led the blonde in by the hand. "Detective, this is Carol, my partner."

"How do you do," Porter said formally, inclining her head. "I'm glad Michelle has someone to support her right now."

"Pleased to meet you," Carol replied, reaching out to shake hands. Her grip was firm. "Michelle has told me about you." Her voice revealed what Michelle had told, and Porter wondered if there was anyone in the world who couldn't tell she was a lesbian.

"Has she." She turned her gaze out the window and noticed for the first time that she could see the upper story of Elaine's house over the trees, across the golf course. It would be nice for Elaine to be there, holding her hand and telling her everything would be all right.

But it wouldn't be. She should have known. She dropped her head. She had screwed everything up. Virginia Williams should have been in custody two days ago, not lying dead in the back of a mortuary van. Porter had failed.

"Christ, you look like someone just shot your dog,"

Joe said, coming in from upstairs. "You ready to go downtown?"

"Yes, I suppose I am." She knew there would be several hours of debriefings to sit through, all the while thinking how she should have handled things differently.

"Ladies," Joe acknowledged the pair standing with Porter. "Miss Williams, I'm very sorry ...."

"Don't be," Michelle replied. "The rest of us can go on living now."

*   *   *   *   *

It was late when Porter got home. She dragged herself over to the bar and fixed a drink, then collapsed onto the sofa and stared moodily at the wall. It took her a minute to realize the light was flashing on her answering machine. Leaning over, she pressed the play button.

"Hi, lover, it's me," Elaine's voice sounded soft, wanting. "Call me when you get in, okay?" The machine beeped. Porter closed her eyes and fought against tears.

A while later, she found herself dialing Elaine's number. It was answered immediately. "Hi," she said tiredly.

"What's the matter?"

"Virginia Williams killed herself." She paused, then filled Elaine in on what had happened. "God, I feel awful."

"Why?" Elaine sounded level, reasonable. "Did she murder her husband?"

"Yes. But I should have known...." Porter felt the misery growing. She longed to be held, but didn't dare ask Elaine to leave the comfort of her house at this hour of the night.

As if reading her mind, Elaine said, "I'll be right over."

"You don't have to – "

"Nonsense. What are friends – or lovers for that matter – for?"

"Are we friends?" Porter hadn't been sure. Lovers, they were, but friendship involved a giving, something she wasn't sure had happened.

"Of course we are."

Twenty-five minutes later, Elaine walked through the door with a bouquet of carnations and a bottle of wine. As Porter stood aside to let her in, Elaine smiled softly and leaned over to kiss her.

"Thank you for coming," Porter mumbled. "I didn't expect...."

Thrusting the flowers at her, Elaine shook her head. "Are you always this moody after a case is finished?"

"No. Only when I lose." Porter took the flowers, feeling slightly foolish. "What are these for?"

"To cheer you up. Same with the wine. How did you lose?"

They moved to the sofa. Porter brought out two

wine glasses and an opener and they settled back against the cushions facing one another. "I've been so preoccupied that I didn't give my full attention to the case. I made mistakes, and a woman is dead because of it."

"What has you so preoccupied?" Elaine grinned over her glass. Porter sighed. It was hard to be morose with Elaine around.

"You do."

"Well, I'll endeavor not to be involved in any more murder cases you're working on. Will that help?" Despite herself, Porter laughed.

"It's a start."

"You're being too hard on yourself. How do you know Virginia didn't plan to kill herself all along? Or kill her children? You figured this thing out in less than a week. I'd say that was damn good." Elaine tugged playfully at Porter's ear. "Am I going to have to take you to bed to cheer you up?"

"Virginia forced Michelle to leave you."

"I know. Michelle came by my office this morning and we had a long talk. The healing will still take some time, but at least now I understand the why."

"You're a very understanding woman." Porter leaned into her, curling her legs up as she snuggled close into Elaine's arms. "I'm glad we're friends."

Elaine stroked her hair. "Maybe we can become more, in time." She kissed Porter's forehead.

"Maybe." Porter didn't know what the future held,

but she was very happy for Elaine's presence in the here and now. She would deal with the aftermath of the case, and the future, tomorrow. Elaine's lips were warm and welcoming, and the best therapy Porter could think of. She allowed herself to become lost in the kiss.

Publications available from
Cape Winds Press, Inc.
PO Box 730428   Ormond Beach, FL 32173-0428
Web Site: http://www.capewindspress.com

We welcome mail orders. Please add 15% for
shipping.

TAHOMA by M. Broughton Boone, 165 pp. Can two
women find happiness in the Washington Territory of
1883?   ISBN 0-9671203-0-6 $12.95

A WILD SEA by Rebecca Montague, 174 pp. A ghost
from the past threatens to destroy a present love.
                ISBN 0-9671203-2-2 $12.95

ALLERGIC REACTION by Leslie Adams, 151 pp.
First in the Debutante Detective series. A country club
beauty with a secret distracts detective Porter Sienna
during a murder investigation.
                ISBN 0-9671203-3-0 $11.95

OFFICE HOURS by M. Broughton Boone, 122 pp. A
Cape Winds Weekend Escape. Will Kaitlan Davis
break her number one rule and get involved with her
boss?   ISBN 0-9671203-4-9 $10.95